His girl friend's father might be the next victim—or had he planned the killing?

The police chief knew more than he was telling—was he protecting his job or a murderer?

The young rebel gang headed by Guru Goat knew what they wanted—but could they shoot fast enough to get it?

Or was it all a private vendetta, triggered by the hatred in one messed-up family?

If Ben had thought more and shot less, he might still be a cop.

But he wouldn't have solved a nasty case of homicide that put his girl friend in deadly danger!

"The author ignites his story on page one and heaps fuel on it all the way to the end."
—New York Times

A
PARLIAMENT
OF OWLS

Patrick Buchanan

▲ PYRAMID BOOKS ● NEW YORK

A PARLIAMENT OF OWLS

A PYRAMID BOOK

Copyright © 1971 by Cork Tree, Inc.

Published by arrangement with Stein and Day Publishers

Pyramid edition published March 1974

ISBN 0–515–03318–9

Printed in the United States of America

Pyramid Books are published by Pyramid Communications, Inc. Its trademarks, consisting of the word "Pyramid" and the portrayal of a pyramid, are registered in the United States Patent Office.

Pyramid Communications, Inc., 919 Third Avenue, New York, N.Y. 10022

For Ray and Flecia Zekauskas for providing the library, the typewriter, and the beer

A PARLIAMENT
OF OWLS

ONE

When we drove up the hill and parked, the killer was already hidden in his ambush, waiting. Below us, the sleepy little New England town stretched out toward the deep blue Atlantic. To the landward side, tree-shaded homes perched on the sloping hillside.

This was Pilgrim's Pride, Massachusetts, at the beginning of a long Fourth of July weekend—the last place in the world you would expect to find violence and death.

"Look, Ben," said Charity Tucker, her long blond hair tossing in the summer morning's breeze. "There's *Channel Nine.*"

In New York City, where I live, Channel Nine is a television station. Here it was a boat—a slender, tall-masted schooner sliding into the harbor below us. Sleek, handsome, it set me to daydreaming. Instead of just being a cop on vacation, I conjured up images of myself as a wealthy playboy, lying on the boat's mahogany deck, a frosty gin and tonic inches away from my bronzed hand.

Charity had spoken of the boat before. It belonged to her father, who, among other ventures, was in the television business. *Channel Nine* was named after the dial setting of his privately owned station.

Watching the boat cut through the outgoing tide, I decided there was absolutely nothing wrong with being rich.

The catch was, I *wasn't* rich. I was just a poor-but-honest New York cop—whose days as a cop were numbered, although I didn't know it then. The ceremonial ripping off of stripes and breaking of swords wasn't due for a couple of days yet.

The schooner left a sparkling bow wave. The Atlantic was the peculiar color of blue you find only in deep water on bright, cloudless days. The water looked cold. I hoped it wouldn't be too frigid to keep me from doing a little lobstering. In the trunk of my beat-up, souped-up old Fleetwood, wrapped in a Navy blanket, was my singletank SCUBA gear. Duty schedules being what they were, I usually managed to use the underwater gear once a year.

I had parked the Fleetwood on a wide curve overlooking the town and its harbor. Directly below, fifty yards or so down the steep slope, a long pier jutted out toward the center of the harbor. The schooner, sails furled, was proceeding under power toward the pier's seaward end.

Isn't she lovely?" Charity said softly, as we stood near the car.

I was turning toward her to make some snappy comeback when I heard a whooshing sound. Without thinking, I tackled Charity and bore her to the rocky ground, my 205 pounds crunching her hipbone against the earth.

I thought I saw something streak across the surface of the water between the land and the schooner. A burst of flame flashed from the side of *Channel Nine*. The boat reared up like a wounded animal and tipped over on its side. One shattered mast slipped off its stump and punched a hole in the deck, then crumpled over slowly, ripping up the boards as it fell.

No one seemed to be abandoning ship.

Charity's hand gripped my shoulder. "Ben! My father's on that boat!"

I scrambled up, trying to decide what to do next.

"Here!" Charity called. I turned around. She had

pulled the keys out of the ignition and was unlocking the trunk. "Your scuba gear."

I ran to help her. When I turned around I could see the schooner shuddering, the water frothing at its gunwales. We watched, horrified, as the boat dipped under the blue surface and disappeared as if some giant hand had pulled it down.

"Hurry, Ben!"

I shouldered the air tank and took off down the hillside with the mouthpiece and regulator banging against my side. Charity followed me, clutching my flippers and mask.

We got down to the pier where a huge bear of a man stood looking out at the roiling water, an expression of complete bewilderment on his face.

"Morning, Miss Charity. Say, did you see that—"

"Seth! Where's your motor launch?"

He gestured toward a ladder over the near edge of the pier. I scrambled down it, dove for the boat's cockpit, and ground the starter button of the inboard engine. It wheezed for a few seconds and then rumbled into life. There was a thump as Charity leaped down into the boat and cast off the stern line. As she hurried to loose the forward mooring, I heard Seth's coarse voice: "You be careful now, you hear, Miss Charity?"

The line splashed into the water and I spun the wheel, heading the launch out toward the place where the schooner had gone down. It wasn't hard to spot: bubbles and bits of debris were still bobbing to the surface.

Charity took the wheel from me as I tore off my shoes and outer clothing. My skivvies were less concealing than a bikini, but this was no time for modesty. As the launch roared closer to the churning patch of water, I slipped into my air tank.

11

I had been wondering whether the water would be warm enough for skin diving. This was the hard way to find out.

After the heat of the July sun, the water was shockingly cold. I felt my heart constrict as the iciness closed around me. I bit down hard on my mouthpiece to keep from losing it. In water this cold, a diver needed a wet suit to survive more than a few minutes.

I followed the stream of bubbles down to the wreck, which lay nearly forty feet beneath the surface. It had left the channel and come to rest in shallower water. I was grateful for that. With every foot I descended, the water got colder.

The boat was rightside up. As I approached it, I saw a terrifying apparition. Like Captain Ahab, one hand pointed upward toward a sun he would never see again, an old, white-haired man stood on the deck, trapped by coils of rope around his legs. His eyes were open and he swayed with the current.

I knew it was too late, but I started to hack him free with the Philippine fighting knife I have carried since Vietnam. I managed to slash one knot free. Then, through a cabin window, I saw the face of a woman.

She appeared to be nearly as old as the man, she was paralyzed with terror—and she was alive. I got over to the window and peered inside. The old woman stood waist-deep in water, gulping breaths of air that had given her a few minutes more of life.

I tapped at the window and pointed down toward the door that lay under the area of the air bubble. She screamed soundlessly and paid no attention to me.

Suddenly the schooner settled to one side. Inside, the woman lurched and fell out of sight. I grabbed the tiller bar and pried at the jammed door. It resisted for a few seconds, then gave way in slow motion. The boat quivered, and the door burst open and hurled me

12

against the deck. Water rushed in, and I knew that unless I moved fast I had freed the woman only to doom her to death by drowning.

Inside the wheelhouse I found her up in one corner of the bulkhead, her nose only inches above the lapping water. As I surfaced just in front of her she started to scream, then seemed to understand why I was there. She said something I couldn't hear. I pulled the mouthpiece of my air regulator from my mouth and inserted it in hers. She caught on and bit down on the rubber. Bubbles spilled out of the regulator as she took a deep breath.

I took the mouthpiece back from her and filled my own lungs before returning it to her mouth. Then I pulled her down into the water and kicked my way toward the dim rectangle of the door. I could feel the icy water sapping my strength. I hoped the old woman's heart would be able to stand the strain.

I had no way of knowing whether or not she knew how to surface properly, letting the air leak out of her lungs to keep the expanding gas from rupturing them. So I took a desperate chance; around the twenty-foot level I gave her a gentle but forceful punch in the stomach and she belched a cloud of bubbles. Before she could suck in the sea water I cupped my hand over her mouth and nose and headed for the surface at top speed, blowing out all the way like a surfacing whale.

I hadn't been down long enough to botch up my bloodstream with nitrogen bubbles. When they explode inside your arteries and tissues, a case of the bends can finish you. Luck was with us both: we surfaced with a minimum of difficulty.

Charity was waiting, leaning anxiously over the edge of the launch. She took one look at the white face of my passenger and yelped, "Granny!" Reaching over, she grabbed the old lady's dress by the collar and heaved while I pushed, and together we tumbled her into the launch as unceremoniously as a sack of bootlegged clams.

I felt the cold closing in on me. Before Charity could say whatever she was going to say, I bit down on my mouthpiece and turned head-down to repeat the agonizing swim to the bottom of the harbor. I fumbled for my knife, and found it tucked neatly into the gaping fly of my skivvies.

It wasn't necessary for me to go all the way to the bottom to free the body of the old man. When the schooner turned over the last time it had ripped the coils or rope lose from his feet.

Now he floated peacefully toward the surface, his head twisted to one side. A school of shad nuzzled up against him, examined him carefully, and departed with a fluttering of tails, disappointed.

I gathered the old man up gently and pulled him toward the dark shape of the launch's hull, which hovered on the surface of the water just above me.

As I surfaced I saw another boat heading right for me. Charity yelled something and it swerved away, just missing me. I passed the old man's body up to two pairs of masculine hands that reached down into the chilly water. Then I grabbed the gunwales and tried to pull myself up.

I couldn't make it. I was so weak that I just hung there with my face under water. I had lost the mouthpiece and was on the verge of sucking in a lungful of salt water when what felt like a pair of iron pincers clamped around my upper arms and yanked me, dripping, out of the ocean and deposited me on the duckboards of the boat.

I spluttered for a little while and then managed to sit up. Two men in water-spattered blue uniforms

14

leaned over the body of the old man. One was pressing his chest in a regular rhythm, attempting to massage his heart back to life. The other held a pulmotor mask over the old man's face. A third, in sport shirt and blue jeans, leaped the gap between our boat and the launch where Charity and her grandmother were huddled.

"Daddy!" she shouted, standing up shakily to hug him. He gave her a quick kiss and bent over the old woman. He ripped off his plaid shirt and wrapped it around her. She looked up and said something I couldn't hear.

I staggered to my knees, then stood up. The two officers paid no attention to me. I looked down at the frail figure of the old man and knew that they were wasting their time.

I stepped over into the boat we'd borrowed. The big man Charity had called "Daddy" looked up from the old woman. His bare chest was covered with curly white hair; he didn't seem to have an ounce of fat on him. He grabbed my arm as I staggered a little and pulled me down into the cockpit with them. Both of us were standing, and though I come in at six-two, I still had to look up to meet his eyes

"You must be Ben Shock," he said. His voice wasn't loud, but it penetrated the splashing of the surf and the grinding engine noises.

One of the uniformed men on the other boat stepped across and nodded at him.

"Lyon," said the uniformed man, "I'm afraid he's gone."

"It's a miracle that either one of them is alive," said Lyon Tucker. "If it hadn't been for Ben Shock here—"

"You did good," the uniformed man told me. He

15

held out his hand. "I heard about you. Mr. Tucker said his daughter was bringing a New York cop up to visit. You ain't exactly what I had in mind."

"Pilgrim's Pride isn't exactly what *I* had in mind," I said right back. He grinned.

"I'm Miles Cooke," he said.

"Harbormaster of Pilgrim's Pride," Lyon Tucker added.

"I didn't see it happen," said Cooke. "I heard the explosion, but by the time I got out of my house she was already going down. Did anyone here see it?"

"I did," I said.

"Any ideas?"

"I've seen other holes like that blown in a boat's hull," I said. "All in Vietnam. All made by a recoilless rifle. Probably around a seventy-five-millimeter."

He frowned. "You mean, a bazooka?"

"Something like a bazooka."

Harbormaster Miles Cooke digested this for several seconds.

"My, my, my," he said finally.

He piled into his own boat and took off. Tucker looked after him.

"Don't get Miles wrong," he told me. "He may not be as highly trained as you New York boys, but he's no dummy, either."

"Yeah," I said. "It takes real talent to be a good harbormaster."

"That isn't what I meant, Ben," said Lyon Tucker. "Miles Cooke is also the Chief of Police of Pilgrim's Pride."

"My, my, my," I said. There didn't seem to be much else *to* say.

TWO

Being a good cop is one of the hardest jobs in the world.

You could say I failed at it: in the end the system licked me and I had to turn in my badge. But until then, I played it as straight as I could. When I was on the midnight shift I never holed up in a secret coop the way eight out of ten did. And while I sometimes had to use my nightstick, I never tried to club out brains or rupture kidneys. If the courts had their way, you'd never use the stick at all. They can afford the luxury of arguing for months about what constitutes excessive force. But as the cop on the beat, I had two seconds to decide whether to bang some wise guy on the head or let him get close enough to use the shapeless object he clutched in his pocket. It might be a knife, a bottle of acid, a gun—and I got exactly two seconds to make up my mind, no instant replays allowed.

I got through those years in uniform and made detective on my own, one member of New York's Finest who did it without political favors from upstairs, without a "rabbi" pulling for me down at headquarters.

I could have used one when I got involved in Charity Tucker's life.

"That girl's a *victim!*" my precinct captain yelled. "You hauled her out from under a rapist! You're a cop, Shock. You aren't supposed to mess around with the victims."

"I don't want to cause any trouble, Captain Murphy," I said. "But this just isn't any of your business."

"The hell it's not my business! There's a lot of heat on already because of your itchy trigger finger. They're calling you gun-happy. They're saying you could have subdued that man without killing him."

"Tell that to the forty-five he was packing," I said. "He tried to blow my head off. What was I supposed to do? Quote him the Weapons Law?"

"You've got a vacation due," said Murphy, slapping his pencil down. "Take it. Get the hell out of town until things cool off."

He was the boss. I cleaned out my locker and telephoned Charity.

"I'm on vaction," I said. "How about coming to my secret fishing lake in the wilds of upstate New York?"

"Counteroffer," she said. "How about spending the glorious Fourth at my family's New England duchy? Lots of four-pound lobsters and ice-cold beer."

So in the wee hours of the morning I launched the Fleetwood onto the East Side Highway. I was still mad at Murphy. By now I should have been used to it, though Cops run in my family. My grandfather was one. My father died in the blue uniform—and two of my brothers carry shields today. I had plenty of experience with the system. But it still made me angry.

Charity stretched herself beside me. She was a vision to make your heart ache—all in white, with her long blond hair pulled back behind her ears. Her eyes were soft with sleep, and she yawned. It didn't matter— nothing she could do could make her ugly.

For the thousandth time, I wanted to reach over and touch her. And for the thousandth time I reminded myself that she was still fighting the memory of the night we had met, when I dragged her, screaming, from beneath the body of the man I'd been forced to shoot. His blood had sheathed her face in red, and it

18

was not until the following day that I saw how young and how beautiful she was.

Ben Shock is a known sucker for good-looking women . . . especially when the woman is as helpless as a fawn wounded by some stupid hunter's misplaced shot.

Charity, who had been the brightest newsgirl at CBS before the attack, hadn't worked since. Hopefully, this long weekend would be good for her too.

We made good time, and it was still early when she pointed toward a cluster of buildings huddled along the coast and said, "That's Pilgrim's Pride." A slender white steeple stood out against the brilliantly blue sky.

Offshore, another object reached into the sky: a lighthouse, with a cluster of strange rods projecting from it.

"Grand Misery Island," Charity explained. "My father uses the lighthouse as an antenna tower."

"And I thought you were a poor working girl."

"Poor enough," she said. "Daddy doesn't believe in spoiling his offspring. He says that when he dies—and there's real doubt that he ever will—I get something, but until then I'm on my own. Which is the way I like it. But my stepbrother is fit to be tied."

"Stepbrother?"

"Leslie O'Hara Tucker. My stepmother's son by her first marriage."

"Divorced?"

"Widowed. Daddy adopted Leslie and his sister, Scarlett." She pointed toward the distant harbor, where a handsome schooner was beating its way against an offshore wind. "I think I see my father's boat coming in."

The road curved down along the edge of a jutting point through a shabby collection of ramshackle

19

houses. On a sign that had originally read, "Welcome to Pilgrim's Pride" someone had crossed out "Pride" and painted in "Shame."

Noticing my glance, Charity said, "Happens every time they replace that sign. This is the part of town nobody likes to talk about. The hippies named it Shame Town; now the people uptown call it that, too, but for a different reason."

I maneuvered the car around a lame, droop-eared dog that ambled across the street. "I'll be damned. You mean to say that little old Pilgrim's Pride has itself a hippie colony?"

"Left over from a music festival some idiot ran up in Rockport," said Charity. "They came, they saw, they crashed right here. And every year, a new batch arrives by thumb."

As I studied the houses, I caught quick flashes of faces looking out at us. Although they were expressionless at this distance, my cop's instinct told me they were hostile as surely as if I had been presented with a signed affidavit.

"We're lucky this heap is so ugly," Charity said. "Otherwise you might get a brick through the windshield."

"Nice place to drive through, but I wouldn't want to stop here," I said.

She grimaced. "I've been after my father to do something about this mess. People shouldn't have to live like this, even if they have copped out. A couple of years back I thought he was going to. There was talk around town of Dad and somebody else going partners in buying up the area and developing it. I asked him and he said there was nothing to it. Then a man named Sam Bramin began gobbling up Shame Town like a pig in a garbage pit. Now the people out here are worse off than ever, and there's real resentment."

Just then a chicken started to run across the road. I hit the brakes and the scrawny bird just made it, but Charity banged her nose lightly on the dashboard. "Thanks," she said, fingering her nose gingerly.

"Sorry," I said. "I didn't want to run over somebody's Sunday dinner."

We came to a railroad crossing and bumped across a double row of tracks. I navigated the Fleetwood around a sharp curve—and suddenly we had entered another world. This part of Pilgrim's Pride was clean and trim and white, movie-set picturesque. I pulled over to the promontory, and as we looked down at the harbor the life I'd led before seemed to fade away and there were only the two of us, a beautiful town, and a blue harbor sparkling in the summer sun. If I believed in premonitions I would say that one touched me then, because I remember thinking as the schooner moved toward us, sails furled, that somehow nothing would ever again be as nice as this.

I was right, but not in the way I thought.

THREE

I slipped into my raincoat like some naked exhibitionist getting ready for a night on the town and, getting into the Fleetwood, followed Chief Miles Cooke's ancient Mercury squad car up the hill. He had given my Caddy a knowing look, cocking his head to listen to its deep-throated exhaust. He didn't have to check under my hood to know I had dual carbs—and I knew from the throbbing hum when he took off that his Merc's engine was not factory-born, either.

Halfway up the hill, a white Continental Convertible cut me off from Cooke. I started to lean on my horn, and then recognized the driver as Lyon Tucker. Charity sat beside him, pale with shock. Tucker stayed in line once he cut in, and we moved along the main drag like a funeral procession—which we were, even though the body was still on the pier awaiting more suitable transportation.

There was something wrong with this town. I could smell it in the air. I could feel it in the tension that seemed to seep in through the half-opened windows of the Fleetwood.

You would expect people to stand and gawk openly at a procession like ours. Instead, they watched from the corners of their eyes. Our route took us through Shame Town. Kids ran out and stared at us. When their parents called them back, they withdrew reluctantly into the ramshackle houses.

As we approached the center of Pilgrim's Pride, I could tell that someone had made a considerable effort to preserve the town as it must have looked two hundred years ago. I wouldn't have been surprised if old Miles Standish himself had suddenly emerged from one of the buildings looking for John Alden. Even the parking meters had the Pilgrim touch; they were shaped like metal turkeys with one long tail feather to activate the instrument. I parked by one of them, got out, and began to scratch around in my pocket for a coin. Chief Cooke came up, shaking his head, and said, "On the house."

The police station, too, looked more like Colonial Plymouth than a working hoosegow. There was even ivy climbing up the outside.

Inside I found that the antique façade was precisely that—a façade. High-efficiency VHF radios and tele-type machines squawked and clattered just inside the entrance. We sat down and started giving our statements. Ordinarily I would have been more observant, but I was wrapped in a wet raincoat and I felt so miserable that all I was thinking about was getting formalities over with so I could get the hell off somewhere to a drink, a shower, and a clean pair of drawers, in that order.

That's why I didn't notice the fat guy with the heavy gold watch chain at first.

"You've got my ID," I told the Chief. "I'm not up here on police business. But when I saw the boat go down, I grabbed my scuba gear and went under to see if I could help."

"And you did help," said Lyon Tucker. "Without you, my wife's mother would be dead."

"I'm just sorry I was too late for the old man."

Tucker sighed. "I am too. But you can't expect miracles. I just wish I'd been on board. I know that ship better than anyone in the world. I might have been able to do something."

That's when I saw Fatso. I gave him the once-over and didn't like what I saw.

No one seemed inclined to question his presence at the proceedings. But it bothered me, and I pointed at him.

"Who's this? The Mayor?"

Cooke laughed nervously. "Oh, my, no, Mr. Shock. May I present Mr. Sam Bramin, one of Pilgrim's Pride's most energetic citizens."

He said it absolutely deadpan, as if he were announcing the presence of God himself. I glanced at him quickly to see if he was putting me on, but his eyes wouldn't meet mine.

Bramin stuck out his pudgy hand. A huge signet ring winked at me from the index finger.

"Heard about the brave thing you did, my boy," he rumbled. He talked like he had been taking elocution lessons from Orson Welles.

"Mr. Bramin is the founder and National Director of the American Defenders," Cooke said.

That placed Fatso for me. I should have pegged him on first sight. His face had appeared on enough magazines and television screens to make him a national figure. As for the American Defenders, they had a well-deserved reputation for being the closest thing to a cross between the Ku Klux Klan and the Nazi Party. I'd encountered their bully boys when the Defenders had held a rally in New York.

Until you attend one of those, you never fully realize how many nuts there are in this world. Would you believe little old ladies in tennis shoes leaping up waving hundred-dollar bills and screaming, "You speak for *us*, Mr. Bramin!"

The worst thing about them was the two-facedness of their definition of democracy. When they didn't agree with what somebody said, they'd fight to the death to keep him from saying it. Anybody they defined as "nonconformist" was regarded with pure, malicious hatred. Naturally, the favor tended to be returned. Now I understood the sullen faces watching silently from the shadowed windows of Shame Town. A bunch of young rebels and the American Defenders living in the same town spelled trouble.

Bramin had come into the national spotlight after buying up two blocks of downtown Detroit which resembled New York's East Village, populated by bearded men and girls with ironed hair. Shortly afterward a party or parties unknown put the houses to the torch, driving out the hippies. A grand jury was still investigating that one, because three of the kids didn't make it out of one of the flaming buildings. The result was a wild riot in which everyone lost except Sam Bramin, who sold the burnt-out blocks at a tidy profit.

A phone rang in the corner, and Bramin was called over to answer it.

"Take that snarl off your face, Ben," said Charity. "Your face would break mirrors."

"I don't blame him," said Lyon Tucker. "Whenever Bramin comes into a room I start wondering how our society can let a demagogue like him exist."

"You've got a voice, Mr. Tucker," I said. "Ten thousand watts of TV signal, if I understand correctly."

He sighed. "Yes, and I've come out publicly against Bramin dozens of times. For what good it does. He's entitled to free equal time to answer me, and I end up giving him a platform to shout his poison from."

"You've also spoken against the hippies," Charity said. "Especially the batch that call themselves Body and Soul."

"Why not?" Tucker answered calmly. "They're just as wrong in their way as Bramin is in his. The Body and Soul bunch make the Weathermen look like bobby-soxers."

"If what I saw of Shame Town is any indication," I said, "they've got plenty to be violent about."

"All they've got to do to afford decent apartments is work a little," he said quickly. "So Charity brought you in by that back road? It's her version of the grand tour."

"Be glad she did. If she hadn't, I wouldn't have been in a position to see your boat go down."

Sam Bramin came over again and laid his hands on both of Charity's shoulders. "This affair is simply dreadful, Miss Charity," he said. "Shocking, disgraceful. But they'll pay, I promise you that. Every resource of the Defenders is at your disposal. We'll bring the dastards"—Yes, he actually said *dastards!*—"to account for their crime."

Lyon Tucker was trying to edge between his daughter and Bramin. And I was tensing up; if Fatso didn't take his hands off Charity pretty quick there was going to be a national incident in the Pilgrim's Pride police station.

Miles Cooke came over and broke up the tableau with bad news.

"Lyon, the hospital just called. Mrs. Garret died ten minutes ago. She had a series of heart attacks and there wasn't anything they could do."

"Oh, terrible!" rumbled Sam Bramin. His paws grabbed out for Charity again, and she flashed me a look of panic. But before I could move, Tucker pulled Bramin away.

"Get your hands the hell off my daughter!" My estimate of him went up six hundred percent.

Bramin spluttered and made a move and then Chief Cooke got between them. I didn't envy the Chief: two of the most important men in his town

26

at each other's throats, and Lucky Miles Cooke in the middle.

Things calmed down, and when we left the station house, Charity got in the white Continental with her father. I followed in the Fleetwood, and we drove up the hill to the Tucker estate.

FOUR

Tucker had quite a place. It looked out over the entire harbor and the ocean beyond it.

The house was old and solid. I'm no expert on such matters, but I had visions of some leathery-faced clippership captain in the late 1800s climbing up this hill, jamming his walking stick into the earth, and shouting out, "Build her here!"

The thought conjured up further visions of riches earned in the Pacific spice-and-silks trade. Or hauling slaves and molasses.

A strange, flat balcony ran along the top of the house, the side that overlooked the sea.

"What's that?" I asked.

"A widow's walk," Charity told me. "It's traditional to have one around here. This place was built by one of the last shipping barons."

Shipping baron! Score one for Shock.

"Slaves?" I said.

Charity shot me a hard look. "Made-goods for California," she said.

Oh, well. One out of two.

We went inside. After walking down an entrance hallway approximately the length of Grand Canyon, we emerged into a living room that could have accommodated a Superbowl game if they'd moved out the expensive furniture.

A gray-haired man in a white jacket asked me politely if he could have my raincoat. Since I had nothing underneath but my skivvies, I declined.

Charity's daddy was obviously doing all right. The

28

furnishings in this room alone must have cost ten thousand bucks. The brace of hand-tooled shotguns hanging over the fireplace had to be worth at least fifteen hundred.

Charity headed straight for the sideboard. Tucker beat her there and said, "Ben, I know you can use a bracer."

"Make it brandy," I said. "That ought to get the circulation moving again."

"Forgive me," he said, turning. "I forgot how uncomfortable you must be. Let me show you to your room and you can change."

"Let's have that bracer first," I said.

Charity brought over a pony that held, at a conservative estimate, five ounces of amber liquid. I swirled it in the glass and sniffed the aroma. It was real stuff. I sipped it appreciatively as Charity went back for her own drink. Lyon Tucker dumped about three fingers of scotch into a tumbler, splashed in warm soda, and downed the whole shebang as if it were ginger ale. He mixed another and stood near a board window that faced the sea, obviously waiting for something.

A door opened. I noticed that the three low steps going up to it also had a sloping ramp along one side. When a young man came in pushing a wheelchair with a woman in it, I understood why.

That can't be Charity's mother, I started to think, and then remembered: she's her stepmother. There was no way to tell how old she actually was. She projected a violent beauty—dark, with high, prominent cheekbones and jet-black, perfectly straight hair drawn back over her shoulders.

Charity rushed up to her, fell to her knees beside the chair, and gave her stepmother a crushing hug.

"Oh, Bethesda," Charity said.

Bethesda Tucker did not answer. She looked over her stepdaughter's shoulder, directly at me.

"Well, well," she said in a deep voice. "Our Charity's got a gentleman caller. Welcome, Mr. Shock. We've heard wonderful things about you."

"Bethesda, there's bad news," Lyon Tucker said sharply. The tone of his voice shocked me. I knew what he was about to tell this woman, and yet there wasn't a trace of warmth about him.

The young man who had been pushing the chair stepped toward Tucker. "Let me tell her," he said. "She shouldn't hear it from you." His voice was crisp and high-pitched.

"Why, Leslie?" Tucker said harshly. "Would you enjoy breaking it to her?"

Leslie. So this was Charity's stepbrother.

"Breaking what, Lyon?" asked the woman.

Tucker walked over and looked down at her. "There was an explosion aboard *Channel Nine* this morning," he said. "She went down instantly. Bart and Nora were aboard. They're both dead. Mr. Shock here got Nora out, but she died later. I'm sorry."

And with that he turned back to the sideboard and poured himself another drink. I wanted to go over and wring his neck.

Bethesda Tucker sat perfectly still, her hands at her throat where they had flown during his toneless announcement. Her words, when they came, were choked. *"And you weren't aboard."*

"Mother," Leslie said in a desperate voice. He looked at her face, then turned on his stepfather. "You bastard!" he shouted. Lyon Tucker didn't even look around. He held up one hand and the boy ran into it and stopped as if he had hit a brick wall. To my surprise, the boy shook off the impact and headed for Tucker again. I started to get up, but Charity nailed me to my chair with a *Don't do it, buddy!* look. So I just sat there and watched.

Before it could turn into a genuine family brawl, Bethesda clapped both hands to her mouth and began to gag.

"Leslie!" Tucker snapped. "Tend to your mother."

The boy lowered his fist and turned. When he saw his mother vomiting through her clenched fingers he ran over, grabbed the chair, and pushed her out of the room.

Charity touched her father's arm. "We'd better go, too," she said.

Tucker lowered his drink slowly without tasting it. His eyes met mine. "Excuse me, Mr. Shock. This is a bad time." He indicated the sideboard. "Help yourself."

I started to tell him to forget it, that I'd come back when things weren't such a mess, but Charity cut me off.

"You stay here, Ben," she said.

They left. I stayed. I finished the gallon or so of brandy Lyon Tucker had given me and got up to pour another quart.

I felt a draft on my neck and turned around. Another set of French doors had opened and through them walked one of the sexiest young women who ever overflowed a bikini. She was dripping wet and left little puddles on the rug as she padded toward me. Her complexion and hair were dark, and it occurred to me that this must have been how Bethesda Tucker had looked when *she* was twenty.

"Glory be," said the girl in a southern accent so thick that it had to be cultivated. "Charity's gone and left her beau to the wiles of little old Scarlett."

I gawked. With some justification. Scarlett—and that actually was her name, it turned out—was exhibiting acres of choicest flesh. And what the suit *did* cover was plainly visible through the wet, almost transparent cloth.

"Do I pass inspection?" she asked, leaning over and plucking the brandy glass from my limp hand.

"All the way," I said softly.

She held out a heavy terrycloth towel. "Dry me," she said, turning her broad back.

As I blotted up the droplets of water, I mentally compared her behind to Charity's. Scarlett's was smaller, rounder, no doubt about that. I decided that still I liked Charity's better.

"How'd you get so wet?" I mumbled.

"In the pool, silly," she said, dripping magnolia blossoms all over me.

"Pool" made me think of water, and water made me think of two old people being dragged to muddy death in the wreck of Lyon Tucker's schooner. It broke the mood.

"Miss Tucker, about your grandparents—"

"I know. It's just awful." Her voice didn't seem to indicate how awful it was. She could have been describing last night's dessert.

"I'm sorry," I told her.

"Maybe it's for the best," she said. "They always said they wanted to go together."

I rubbed around with the towel and found what I'd expected. The front panel of the bra was somewhere down around Scarlett's waist and her high breasts were fair game for my hands. I felt the nipples harden against my palms and waited for her to react.

She fooled me. She didn't show any sign that I was even in the same room. Feeling a little disgusted with myself, I took my hands away, finished drying her, and threw the soggy towel over her shoulder.

"Thank you very much, Mr. Shock." She turned

calmly and looked me in the eye without a trace of embarrassment. The towel fell strategically over most of her superstructure. Most but not all.

I mumbled something that came out like "Gawk, ah, fawp, and she gave me a big Crest smile.

"I guess you'll be seeing more of me, Shock. A lot more."

Then she turned and switched away. Take the word of an expert bikini-watcher: there are very few broads in this world who can walk away from you while wearing one. Scarlett O'Hara Tucker was one of them.

I slopped some more brandy into the pony and poured it down as Charity and her father came back into the room. She was walking very close to him, and he was obviously explaining something in an earnest voice.

"I can't help it, Elizabeth," he said. "Situations like that are my blind spot. I can't think of anything to say, and when I say something it comes out rough."

"I understand," she said. "But I don't think Ben did. And I'm certain Leslie didn't."

Lyon Tucker came over to me.

"I apologize," he said. "The last thing I want is for you to be involved in a family scene. I'm afraid I'm not very good in spots like that."

I shrugged. "I think you handled it about as bad as it could have been done."

"I know," he said. He turned away from me with a little gesture of his big hands that made him look strangely vulnerable.

"Your stepson's the one you have to convince, not me," I said. "He looked as if he would enjoy nothing more than taking you apart to see what holds the pieces together."

Tucker poured himself another scotch. "That's

nothing new," he told me. Charity went over to the window and stared down at the harbor; her father and I sat down on the ten-foot-long couch.

"Bethesda is my second wife, you know. My first died some years ago. I remarried a couple of years later. Leslie and Scarlett came with that marriage." He looked over his scotch at me. "You haven't met Scarlett."

"We've met," I said. Charity gave me a sharp look.

He sipped his drink. "Well, as is often the case in a mixed family like this, one of the stepchildren—Leslie—thinks I favor Elizabeth over him and his natural sister. I've never consciously done so, but Leslie acts as if I have."

"What does Scarlett think?" I asked.

He laughed. "Who knows what Scarlett thinks about anything? She's the one I understand least."

"She's not so hard to understand, Daddy," said Charity. "I bet Ben understands her."

"I only said hello," I said lamely, then changed the subject: "Mr. Tucker, I'm out of my home territory here, but I'm familiar with homicide cases. Maybe I could give Chief Cooke a hand."

"Homicide?" he said numbly. "Yes, it *is* homicide, isn't it?"

"Somebody put a high explosive round from a recoilless rifle into your schooner," I said. "And it would be sensible to consider the possibility that they thought *you* were aboard at the time."

"I don't think you'd better mix in," he said slowly. "We're a very insular community here, Ben. You'd only stir up resentment. I have faith in Miles Cooke. I think he's smart enough to call Boston if he needs help."

"Your decision," I said.

We talked a while longer, then Charity went to her

34

room for a nap while I changed and went up on the widow's walk to relax in the heat of the mid-afternoon sun. Some vacation!

That evening Charity and I drove up to Rockport for a lobster dinner. It was a bundle of laughs. We tossed down martinis like they were going out of style and picked at our food and snarled at each other. I wanted to grab her up in my arms and tell her everything was all right, that old Ben would fix the hurt— but the invisible web that can bind a man and woman together when things are going well had been severed tonight.

It's really going to be a grand and glorious Fourth, I thought as we drove home.

The white-haired servant let us in. "Paul, this is Mr. Shock," Charity said. "Paul came with us from California," she explained.

Paul nodded. "I've met Mr. Shock," he said. "I want to thank you, sir, for what you tried to do. Those poor old folks." He held out his hand and I took it. His thanks sounded more calculated to impress than genuine. But then, condolences usually are.

Bedtime was early this evening. Charity and I had one drink together and sat for a few minutes on the widow's walk, looking down at the specks of light scattered around the harbor. The moon wasn't up yet and the sky looked black and greasy.

I kissed her goodnight and it was like kissing a department-store dummy. She didn't pull away but neither did she respond. I put my arms around her and she pressed up against me for a few seconds and I could feel wetness against my cheek. Then she broke away and ran inside. I lit a cigarette and waited there for a decent interval to give her time to avoid a hallway confrontation, then went to my room, undressed, and got into bed.

It had been a long, long day. My duty tour in the city last night seemed a million years ago. Was it only this morning that I'd signed out, picked up Charity, and set out for a holiday in Massachusetts? It seemed as if I had spent my entire life in Pilgrim's Pride.

There was a faint odor of jasmine in the room. I wondered who had lived in it before? Bethesda's parents? That was a creepy thought, and I tried to put it out of my head.

Outside, the wind blew a tree branch against the shutters. It made little whispering sounds, like a cat scratching to get in. I listened for a while and began to doze.

A light fell briefly across my face. The door to the hallway had opened and closed. I rolled over and my hand dived for the .38 Police Special I'd put on the floor beside the bed.

"Shhh," said a voice. It was Charity.

"Don't you ever knock?" I grumbled. "That's a good way to get yourself shot."

The bed sagged as she sat down near my shoulder. I could smell the rich warmth of her body and a faint wisp of perfume. I fumbled for my cigarettes, found them, and lit one. The match flared and threw angry black shadows into the corners of the room.

In a little girl's voice, Charity asked, "Can I have one?" I pushed the pack at her and lit the cigarette she put to her lips.

"Ugh, menthol," she said. "Don't you have any with tobacco in them?"

"You want special brands, lady, bring your own."

We sat there and puffed silently for a while. Involuntarily my hand crept around her waist. She stiffened slightly at first, then relaxed.

"Well," I said after a long time, "ain't we got fun?"

Charity started to giggle. I tickled her and she giggled some more. She pushed my hand away from her short ribs and somehow it got stuck between her thighs for a moment; her flesh was so warm that I felt as if I had been burned. I took my hand away and put it on her knee instead. She let it rest there.

"Ben," she said, "my father's scared to death. I've never seen him like this before."

"I don't blame him. He could have been on board that boat when it got hit."

"Not that kind of fear," she said thoughtfully. "He's a very brave man when it comes to physical things like pain and death. No, this is something else."

"What?"

I felt her shrug. "I don't know. Ben, I know Daddy told you to stay out of this. But if I asked you very nicely, would you mix into it?"

"Baby," I said truthfully, "if you asked me to walk across the harbor on my size tens, I'd give it a try."

'I know this was supposed to be a vacation," she said. "But I'm so frightened for Daddy. I'll make it up to you, Ben."

"Promises, promises," I said, trying to turn it into a joke. She didn't hear it that way.

"I mean it," she said. The thin sheet rustled as she slid her body under it. I felt her warmth against me and realized at the same moment that—as usual—I was sleeping raw.

"Hey, baby," I said. "I was only joking."

"I wasn't," she said. She wrapped her arms around my neck, and her lips pressed up against mine. Moral I may be, but stupid I am not. I kissed her back—hard. Her lips softened against mine and for a moment it seemed that the hangup between the two of us had vanished.

But the moment was all too brief. Charity gasped and her hands tightened around my shoulders. She was pressed against the entire length of my body. Her hips moved against mine and then she began to squirm. I thought she was trying to get closer to me. But it soon because obvious that she was trying to get away. I relaxed my grip on the gentle curve of her back.

She sat up and her feet thumped on the floor. I heard her breath rasp as she tried to keep from crying.

"Oh, Ben, I'm sorry. I just *can't*."

I stroked her hair. "I know, baby. It's all right."

"No it's not. It isn't fair. I led you on and now I—" She stopped. When her voice came again it sounded miserable. "I'm not a tease. Really."

"Come on, sweetheart," I said. "It's not all that serious. I appreciate the compliment. I really do. There's no hurry, we've both got plenty of time."

It was supposed to cheer her up. Instead she began to bawl as if her heart were breaking. She bent over and planted a wet, smacking kiss on my cheek and spilled a few teardrops down my neck. Then she broke for the door and left me there in the dark, feeling like a heel for not knowing what to do next.

The tree branch rustled against the window for a long time before I managed to go to sleep. When I finally did, I dreamed about Captain Ahab and his goddamned white whale.

FIVE

The next morning after breakfast, I drove down the hill to see Chief Miles Cooke. In the excitement of the previous day I hadn't noticed the sign that hung over the arched door: "PILGRIM'S PRIDE GAOL"!

It was a wonder the city fathers and the Chamber of Commerce didn't have poor Miles decked out in a floppy hat, Pilgrim collar, and silver-buckled shoes. Holding a flared-end blunderbuss.

He seemed glad to see me.

"Sorry this mess is the first impression you get of our town, Mr. Shock," he said.

"Forget it. As you know, I don't have any jurisdiction up here. But it's been suggested that I might come in handy acting as sort of a go-between."

I didn't indicate that it was Charity, not Lyon Tucker, who had suggested the arrangement.

"Sounds all right to me," said Cooke.

"Did any other witnesses come forward?"

He held up a sheaf of Xeroxed papers. "Copies of statements. You're welcome to look through them. I didn't find anything that helped. But you might pick up something I missed."

I was glad to hear him talk this way. Apparently he wasn't going to get his back up like many small-town cops do when the "expert" from the big city arrives.

"There's an empty desk over there," he said. "Boy who used it is in the hospital. Mumps." He gave a short laugh. "The rest of us put such a run on the gamma globulin that they had to ship more down from Boston. You're welcome to use the desk while you're in town."

Before I could thank him the door burst open and a scuffling, shouting melee erupted into the room. Two uniformed figures yelled for help. Cooke and I moved in and pulled two overalled men away from a long-haired young man they were trying to strangle.

"Hold it!" Cooke shouted. "What the hell's going on here?"

The cops and the two overalled men all started to talk at once. The long-haired man said nothing. One of his eyes was almost closed and a trickle of blood ran down from the left nostril. I got him by the arm and pulled him over to a bench out of range of the other two men. He gave me a frightened stare but still didn't say anything.

"Everybody shut up!" Cooke shouted. The babble of voices stilled. Cooke pointed at one of the cops, a short, ruddy-faced man. "You, Harper," he said. "What's the beef?"

"We were coming back from a run down the coast," said Harper. "The bus was crossing over the railroad tracks into the main part of town when we caught up with it. And—"

Cooke closed his eyes slowly, reopened them. "What bus?" he asked.

"The bus the fight was happening on," said the cop. "You know, the bus that runs through Shame Town."

"This hippie thought he was gonna ride right on into Pilgrim's Pride," one of the men blurted out.

"Did I ask you to say anything?" Cooke drawled. "Shut your trap."

The overalled man obliged.

"The bus driver honked his horn at us and we pulled him over," said Harper. "These two guys"—He indi-

40

cated the men in overalls—"were trying to throw him out the bus window."

"Okay," Cooke said. "Lock 'em up."

"Wait just one goddamned minute," said the man who had been silent. "You ain't heard our side of it."

"Mister," Cooke said, "I'm not interested in your side of it. You've got one phone call coming. You'd better call your lawyer." He turned to the desk sergeant. "Book them on Disorderly Conduct until we get something better."

"I don't want no lawyer," said one of the men. "I want to talk to Sam Bramin."

"I figured you would," Cooke said. He nodded toward a door in the back of the station house. "Take them back there," he told the two policemen. "Let them make their calls and then fill out your charge sheets."

"Why waste the paper?" asked Harper. "You know it won't stick. It never does."

Cooke stepped over to the long-haired young man. "You'll make a complaint, won't you, son?" he asked.

The youth looked up, and shook his head slowly.

"I don't want any trouble," he said. "I wouldn't have stayed on that bus except I fell asleep and missed my stop."

"That still doesn't give these punks any call to beat up on you," said Cooke. "If you won't stand up for your rights, there's not much I can do to help you."

"I don't want trouble," the young man repeated. "Look, I just want to go my way without any heat. I don't belong to Body and Soul. I work for a living. Ask Mrs. Simpson at the rooming house."

"Sure," Cooke muttered. "Chuck," he said to the desk sergeant, "see that this man's treated at the emergency ward and then give him a ride home.

Use an unmarked car. This citizen doesn't want any trouble."

"Whatever you say," said the desk sergeant.

Cooke started toward the main entrance. I followed him outside.

"Stuffy in there," he said. "Let's get some coffee."

I didn't particularly want coffee, but I did want to talk to him. So I went along to the diner across the street and tried my luck with a brew that came in a mug heavy enough to break your toe.

Shock's Law about diner coffee is simple: If sparks leap from the spoon to the nearest metal, don't drink what's in the cup. Put it in your car battery instead.

Pilgrim's Pride had a slightly better grade of brew. It went the other direction from the battery-acid route: weak and watery. Chief Cooke didn't seem to mind. He slurped away at the coffee as if he actually enjoyed it.

"Bad stuff," he said. Since the nod of his head indicated the police station instead of the coffee cup, I figured he was referring to the assault incident.

"The times they are a-changing," I said.

"You're telling me," he growled. "But dammit, it's not my fault. Take that guy they were beating up. If he'd make a complaint, I could put them away for a while on Assault. This way the best I'll be able to do is Disorderly, and the judge'll slap their wrists and give them a suspended. Why the hell won't that kid stand up for his rights?"

"Like the man said, maybe he doesn't want trouble."

Cooke motioned for another cup of the witch's brew. "Yeah," he said. "You're right. They could make life miserable for him."

"Who's 'they'?" I asked.

Involuntarily he glanced around to make sure no one was within earshot. "I can't prove anything," he said. "But five'll get you ten it's Bramin's crowd."

"The American Defenders?"

He nodded. "Things were pretty calm here before the Defenders moved in. Now there's nothing but trouble. You've got the Defenders on one side of town and that militant hippie outfit, Body and Soul, on the other. And a lot of kids, like that one, in the middle."

"I can believe there's trouble," I said.

"I'm sitting on a box of dynamite. Sometimes I wake up at night and hear the fuse sizzling." He gulped down the rest of his coffee, got up, and tossed a half-dollar on the counter. As we walked across the street, he filled me in on the rest of the story.

When Bramin's American Defenders first began harassing the hippies who at that time were living moderately quietly in the community, the ordinary people of Pilgrim's Pride rose to their defense. For a while it looked as if Bramin would be defeated by common decency.

Then a hippie leader who called himself Guru Goat appeared with a large collection of followers—Body and Soul. This new group went out of their way to seek confrontation. Pilgrim's Pride, unknown to anyone except travel agents, suddenly made headlines when a six-day riot brought out the National Guard. When the smoke cleared, the railroad tracks had become the unofficial boundary between the Defenders and the hippies.

Now both forces were spoiling for another fight, with the ordinary townspeople caught in the middle.

Miles Cooke ground the starter of his Merc and the souped-up motor under the hood rumbled into life. Tires squealed against the pavement, and my head snapped back as we blasted off.

43

"One nice thing about being the Law," he said. "You can drive a hotrod and get away with it."

"I know what you mean," I said. Both of us fell silent.

"Where are we going?" I asked after a few minutes.

"Kirby's Boatyard. We had the dredge out there this morning and brought up most of the Tucker boat. Figured you'd like to look it over."

I leaned back and lit a Kool. This man was all right. He had a few soft edges, particularly his molly-coddling of Sam Bramin, but other than that he seemed to be playing it straight.

Channel Nine lay on her side, her hull buckled and splintered. The seaweed and barnacles indicated she had needed a bottom job. Now there was no point to it.

Kirby, a tall, cadaverous man in his late fifties, beckoned us over to the hull.

"Take a look," he invited. He pointed at a gaping hole near the boat's stern. "Something went through right here. Then it exploded inside and blew the hell out of everything. She must have gone down like a rock."

"She did," I said.

"You're the cop from New York?" I nodded. "Good try," he said. "That water's damned cold."

"How do you know it happened the way you said?" I asked.

Kirby showed me a cardboard box full of wood scraps. "There's impact marks on the ends of some of these planks," he said. "And blast marks on the inside. Add that to the way they were ripped outward, and you arrive at what I said."

"Any metal?" I asked.

He nodded, went into his shack for a moment. He returned with a bushel basket full of metal scraps, most of which seemed to be pieces of the shattered engine. One jagged, twisted shape caught my eye. I slanted it against the light and found a few numbers embossed on its surface.

I handed it to Miles Cooke. "That's part of the fuse section from a seventy-five-millimeter recoilless rifle shell," I said.

"You sure?"

I nodded. "I've seen enough of them," I said. "Who's got that kind of hardware around here?"

"Maybe the National Guard over to Gloucester," he said.

I sensed he wasn't telling me everything. "Come on, Chief," I said. "We both know the National Guard wasn't using *Channel Nine* for target practice."

He hesitated. "I can't prove it," he said finally, "but a fairly reliable informant over in Shame Town told me he'd heard Body and Soul were shipping in some heavy weapons."

"Jesus Christ!" I exploded. "And you didn't check it out?"

"How would *you* check out a story like that?"

"Get my informant closer to the action."

"That's what I asked him to do. I haven't heard from him since."

That shut me up. We stood around for a while, kicking stones and looking at the broken hull. Then he drove me back toward town.

"Why would Body and Soul want to take a potshot at Lyon Tucker?" I asked.

Cooke shrugged. "He'd been pretty harsh with them on the air."

"Hasn't he been even harder on the Defenders?"

"Maybe. But every time he comes out against *them*, Sam Bramin gets equal time to answer."

"And Body and Soul doesn't?"

"If they're offered it, they don't use it. I can't remember them ever coming on to talk back."

"Where would I find this leader of theirs, Guru Goat?"

The Merc screeched to a stop on the hill.

"You don't," said Cooke. "You're just a private citizen, Shock. You've been some help and I appreciate it. But don't go messing around where you don't belong."

"Even a private citizen is allowed to talk to another private citizen," I said.

He snorted. "Try it. You'd be surprised how many little ordinances a stranger can violate in a town like this. We'll run you in every time you spit on the sidewalk."

I got out of his car. It was suddenly crowded in there. "Yeah," I said, "a cop's got plenty of ways to put the heat on troublemakers. That's what's got me wondering."

"Wondering what?" he asked.

"Why you didn't use some of those tricks on your *real* troublemakers. Like Guru Goat. And Sam Bramin."

"Shock, you talk too much."

"And you don't talk enough," I said. I started walking up the steep road. In a minute or so the Merc pulled up beside me and kept pace. I glanced over. Cooke was practically blowing steam out of his ears.

"Don't worry, Chief," I called. "I won't spit on the sidewalk. Or even walk on the grass."

He cursed and hit the gas. But when the big car was around twenty yards ahead of me he changed his mind and screeched the brakes. As I caught up, he leaned over and opened the right front door.

"Get the hell in," he said. "You'll get sunstroke out there."

46

I grinned and slid onto the seat. We drove on. Nobody talked for a while.

"Guru Goat hangs out in the old Bijou Theater," he said, looking straight ahead. "We've rousted him a couple of times, but it didn't do any good."

"Does he run Body and Soul from there?"

"More or less. But whatever he's got in the way of weapons, he must keep somewhere else. We've searched that crummy theater from top to bottom."

We pulled up outside the ornate "Gaol" and I got out.

"Thanks," I said.

"Watch your ass," he said. "Those are rough people."

"I will," I said. I went over to my parked Fleetwood and got in. Charity was sitting in the front seat.

"Morning," I said.

"You were up early," she said.

"The early bird catches the worm."

"My aren't we bright and witty."

"Charity, my love, I adore you too much to invite you to join me for coffee in yonder poisonery. What do you say we go back to your place for some breakfast?"

"I've had breakfast," she said. "But I'll watch you eat some."

I sighed. "I've already paid a visit to Chief Cooke's favorite diner. My stomach may be out of action for keeps. But I'll drop you off at home, and—"

"Where are you going?"

"No place special."

"Good. I'll go there with you."

"Like hell you will."

"Like hell I won't."

We kept that up for a few minutes and then I drove off toward Shame Town with her sitting beside me, as I had known all along she would be. In New

York, Charity Tucker had been known as a gal who was always out in front, walking wherever the danger was. In a way, that made her present fears more pathetic. I knew she was trying to prove something to herself by coming with me, and I couldn't bring myself to turn her down.

We cruised around the depressing streets of Shame Town until the weatherworn Bijou Theater appeared off our port bow.

There is nothing sadder than an abandoned theater. Most small towns have two or three—palaces of joy that have gone to ruin. They sit crumbling on side streets, their box offices boarded up, and the display cases that once sheltered Greta Garbo and Clark Gable from the rain are broken and paint-peeled.

In New York City, these obsolete arenas are often turned into supermarkets. I have often wondered if, late at night, inventory clerks are ever startled by the whispering of long-dead voices. . . *"Men, we're going to hold Wake Island!"* . . . *"Jimmy, I won't let you break up the act. We—we're a team!"* . . . *"Doctor Transylvania never should have tampered with the forces of life. There are some things Man is not meant to know!"*. . . and, of course, *"Frankly, my dear, I don't give a damn!"*

Which started me to wondering what Charity's well-endowed stepsister Scarlett was doing today. . . .

We parked around the corner, off the main street. If there were any bearded faces in the windows looking down on the chipped asphalt street, I didn't see them.

The Bijou had obviously been closed a long time. Tattered posters advertising Betty Hutton in *The Greatest Show on Earth* were still hanging on inside the display cases. As I'd expected, the glass was long gone, and so were the once-garish colors of the posters.

You could barely make out the grim jaw of Charlton Heston.

The double doors to the theater lobby were slightly ajar.

I suggested that Charity wait in the car. She suggested that I blow it out my ear.

I stuck my head inside the door.

"Hey," I yelled. "Anyone home?"

"Nobody here but us chickens," answered a voice.

Ask a stupid question . . .

I stepped inside, Charity right on my heels.

The air was moist and smelled of mold. The tiny lobby was separated from the theater by a partition. I went around it. A single aisle stretched down an incline toward the small stage, which was dimly lighted by a bare bulb hanging from the flies.

Under it, his feet perched up on a milk crate, a man sat. His face was turned toward us.

I was on the stage before I could see what he looked like. He had long hair, and wore a thin little beard that made him look like a billy goat. His clothes were all of leather.

Something clicked behind me. I glanced over. Charity had slipped a mini-camera out of her purse and was palming it, clicking off exposures of the man on the stage.

"My name's Shock," I said. "I'm looking for Guru Goat."

"Go ahead and look."

"I'm a friend of the Tuckers," I told him. "It won't come as any surprise to you that someone blasted Lyon Tucker's boat out of the water yesterday. His wife's parents were killed."

"Tough," he said.

I tried a feint. "What did Body and Soul have against those old people?"

"Nothing," he said. "It's Lyon's lying ass we want. Those poor innocent bystanders—" He stopped and stood up slowly. "Tricky, aren't you?"

"Why do you have it in for Tucker?" I asked. "I'd think Sam Bramin would be on top of your hate list."

"Man, you've got a big mouth," he said. "Why don't you take it and your blond friend out of here before you get hurt?"

I felt a flush of anger as he turned toward Charity.

"Get going, yellow bird," he laughed. "Or the boogey man will *eat* you!"

I took a step toward him. His hands swooped out in my direction and I saw the flash of a knife blade.

I didn't want to draw my .38 on him to make him drop the knife. I dipped into my pocket and came up with my Philippine fighting knife. A sergeant from Luzon taught me to use the weapon in Vietnam, and I've carried it ever since. The blade is cradled inside two splits of wood that form a carrying case. As you whirl the weapon into action, they separate and become the handle. You could shave with the blade— and, on occasion, I have.

"You better know how to use that thing," said the man, "or you may wind up talking in a very squeaky voice."

"It's *your* voice I'm interested in," I said "Start off by telling me what your gang has against Lyon Tucker."

"Make me," he said.

We circled each other. He feinted at me, and I parried his blade with my own.

"Ben!" Charity called. "Out there!"

My eyes, now accustomed to the dimness, picked out several shadowy figures slipping down the aisle.

I looked around. On one side of the stage, cracks of light indicated the location of one of the fire exits. I shoved Charity toward it. Then, as the men leaped up onto the stage, I slashed savagely with the fighting knife.

The first man leaped back. But it wasn't him I was after. My blade found the dangling wire of the work light, and with a flash of sparks the bulb dropped to the stage and shattered.

The floorboards trembled as the newcomers rushed to where I had just been. By then I was pressed against the exit door.

"Ready?" I asked Charity.

She pressed my arm, and I threw open the exit. The bright sun splashed in, revealing a group of men stumbling over each other on the stage. We hustled out onto the street. I dove into the driver's seat of the Fleetwood and jabbed the key into the ignition.

"Here they come," Charity said calmly. She rolled up the windows and pressed down the door locks. I ground the starter, pumped the gas—too—fast and flooded the carbs.

The door locks didn't stop the men from trying to rip up the hood and get at the distributor wires. But it was doubled-locked, and they got nowhere.

The man we'd "met" on the stage picked up a brick and smashed it against the window next to Charity's face.

She screamed as the safety glass cobwebbed. The man hefted the brick for another try, and then the engine caught. Another man crawling over the hood to get at the windshield rolled off as I hit the gas. My rear window went opaque white as the first man heaved his brick at it. We were off and running.

"Nice place to drive through," I said, my heart pounding.

"But I wouldn't want to stop there," Charity finished.

We drove the rest of the way without saying a word.

SIX

Crossing the railroad tracks into Pilgrim's Pride was like getting back to base in Vietnam after a midnight patrol. The air seemed suddenly fresher; the sun, brighter; the world, friendlier. But I knew that this wasn't so. . . .

Charity took out her cigarette-lighter-sized camera and wound a couple of knobs. She clicked out a tiny black cassette. "I think I got some good ones," she said, examining the cassette. "This thing is loaded with Kodak's new Four-X negative. I can push it to two thousand ASA if I develop by inspection."

"Bully," I said. "Kodak I understand. The rest was Greek."

"Why did you ask him that question about my stepmother's parents?" she said, sliding the cassette into her breast pocket. It made an unsymmetrical lump that was vaguely irritating.

I shrugged. "Sometimes the direct way is the best. Anyway, it worked."

She looked at the shattered window an inch from her cheek. "And it almost got you killed, too."

"He wasn't going to kill anybody," I said, wishing I was as sure about that as I hoped I sounded.

"Or worse," she went on. "That remark about your speaking in a high voice."

"Just a lot of talk to scare me off." The lie tasted sour. Whatever the man on the stage had meant—to kill or not to kill—he had the unmistakable look of a knife fighter who likes to go for the crotch.

"You can press charges against him, can't you?"

53

I shook my head. "No witnesses."

"I'm a witness."

"No, honey. Both of us were trespassing. That's our friend's story, anyway, and we'd play hell breaking it down."

We didn't say anything to each other for a while. Then she said, "Ben, drop me at the police station."

"Why?"

"I want to use their lab to develop these negatives."

"Will they let you?"

"If I flirt a little with their technician. He's a real photo bug anyway, and he secretly hopes I'll hire him away from here to shoot newsreels for CBS. And as long as I'm there, I want to look over the reports on the explosion."

"I went through them all, hon," I said. "Dry holes."

"Maybe," she said. "But I might see something you missed. After all, I know the town better than you do."

"So does Chief Cooke. And he went over them."

"Listen, buster," she said, "I'm going to look at them anyway, so why don't you stop griping."

"And I thought *I* was the cop in this car."

"Can it!" she snapped. "You're just afraid I'll find something you *men* missed!"

She was right. This wasn't the first time I'd found myself resenting Charity's intrusion into what I regarded as my turf.

"I'm sorry, honey," I said, "You're right. Go ahead and look."

She was too mad to accept my apology gracefully, but at least she stopped kicking her foot against the firewall.

"While you're working on the reports," I said, as we pulled up outside the police station, "I want to talk to your father."

"He's probably at the TV station."

54

"Out there in the lighthouse?"

"No, that's just the transmitter. The station's on the mainland about a mile south of here. Just follow the main highway and take the bypass around Shame Town."

That suited me fine. I'd had enough for one day of windows with hostile faces behind them.

I gave her a quick peck on the cheek; she hopped out, trotted up the steps, and went inside. I jockeyed the big car into the police parking lot to turn it around and almost ran over Charity's stepsister, Scarlett.

"Watch it," she drawled, leaning against my door. "Molest me, and I'll call a cop."

"I *am* a cop," I said.

"Do tell," she said. "Well, I was just going to hail a taxi. But now that you're here, I won't have to do that, will I?"

I sighed. "No, ma'am," I said. "My carriage is at your disposal, Miss Scarlett."

She got in, registering surprise at the cobwebbed windows.

"Bats," I informed her in my best cornpone accent. "Poor critters can't see where they're going in the daylight and they just bash their foolish little bodies to pieces against this big old car."

She made an impatient gesture. "Can you drop me off at the TV station, Mr. Shock?" This time her southern accent was completely gone and she sounded mean.

"Consider it done," I said, wheeling out onto the street and heading south.

In clothes, Scarlett looked just as sexy as she had in her bikini. She wore blue jeans that were about three sizes too small and a light blue work shirt with the tail flopping out. The jeans were obviously designed for a boy, and the glittering metal of the zipper only emphasized her femininity.

"How come you got stranded at the station house?"

She patted a flat envelope that stuck out of her purse. "Daddy has to sign some papers. About the—murders. They weren't ready when we drove in, so I waited while he went on out to the TV station."

"That's where I'm headed," I said.

"Do you know how to get there?"

"More or less. I'm supposed to look for the bypass."

"I know a better way," she told me. "Turn right at that next stop light."

A little alarm bell went off, but I ignored it.

"Are you disturbed about something, Mr. Shock?" she asked as the road led us up the hillside above the town.

"Me? No, not a bit," I lied. "Look, call me Ben. Everybody else does."

"My name is Scarlett. My mother had this hangup on *Gone With The Wind*."

"I thought so," I said lamely. Our conversation reminded me of a scratched record. A lot of words were being said, but a recurring "click" kept telling me that underneath it all something was very wrong.

We reached the top of the hill and turned south again.

"Pull into that dirt road up there on the left," Scarlett said.

I nosed into it and as it tilted downhill, the trees and brush closed in tightly. Branches scraped against the top of the car. A hundred yards father down the narrow road we were totally isolated from the rest of the world.

Then the road widened into a sort of parking area, with heavy logs stretched along the downhill side. The hill dropped sharply away beyond the logs, and the view of the harbor and the ocean was breathtaking.

"Beautiful, isn't it?" Scarlett said.

I agreed.

"Ben," said Scarlett, leaning over, "I know how kind you've been to Charity, and I just want you to know it's appreciated."

She demonstrated by kissing me. It started out one of those "You're a nice guy and I like you" kisses, but as the seconds ticked by we left the friendship route far behind. Her mouth tasted of rose-flavored lipstick and at first her lips were cool and firm, but then they loosened. I pulled away and made a big deal out of fiddling with the car radio, justly considering myself to be a hero above and beyond the call of duty.

"I saw her last night, you know," Scarlett said.

"Saw who?" I mumbled, trying to concentrate on the radio.

"Charity. She went into your room just after midnight and I thought, aha! But she came out too soon for anything to have happened."

"She just wanted to say goodnight," I said.

"Is that why she was crying?"

I didn't answer.

Softly, she said, "Maybe you ought to try another Tucker." Her hand crept over and stroked the inside of my leg. A thrill shot up my groin and into my stomach.

What the hell, why not? Charity and I hadn't sworn any vows of loyalty. I let my hand slide inside the gaping neckline of her shirt. Her breasts were bare, and warm against my fingers.

"You won't be sorry," she whispered. "I'm ever so much better than she is."

"How do you know?"

She pouted. "It's a small town," she said. "The boys compare notes."

I took my hand away. "And do you always make it a point to come around later and give the guys a chance with the other Tucker?"

"Why not?" Scarlett said. "She's always had everything her own way. She's got her career and Daddy makes no bones about the fact that she's the darling apple of his eye. Well, there's one thing I can beat her at. Ask anybody."

"No thanks," I said pushing her away. I felt sick. I was disgusted with myself, and I turned it on her. "You stupid little bitch, don't you realize that your sister has been through something that's pushed her to the edge of the loony bin?"

"So what?" she said. "It wasn't being raped that sent her off. It was learning that she *liked* it!"

"She told you that?"

"She didn't have to," Scarlett said.

"And," I said, "you've passed the news to everyone in town."

She gave me a tight smile. "Only to those who would be interested," she said. "Only those who know she's been playing Miss Purity up here while she'll spread her legs for any—"

That was as far as she got. I hit her—hard—with the back of my hand. Scarlett didn't even flinch. Her lower lip started to puff immediately.

"You bastard!" she hissed.

"I'm sorry," I said, meaning it. "But you shouldn't have said those things."

"I'll get you for this."

"I'm sure you will," I said, handing her my handkerchief. She threw it back in my face.

"Let's go," she said. "I'm used to being hit. When

58

you big heroes can't get it up, you always use your fists. It makes you feel like *men*."

I turned the car around and drove up the narrow road. In a few minutes we were coming down the hill toward the TV station; a small complex of neat white buildings set deeply into a cliff directly over the ocean.

Lyon Tucker's Continental was parked in the lot beside four other cars and one panel truck marked WRKA, CHANNEL NINE, PILGRIM'S PRIDE, MASS.

Scarlett was out of the car before I had the motor turned off.

"Sweat, you bastard," she said. "You'll pay for this."

I didn't say anything. I wasn't especially proud of myself. I sat there with the midday heat shimmering off the asphalt of the parking lot, and lit a cigarette. It tasted like old lettuce. I threw it down and went inside.

The receptionist told me to have a seat. A couple of minutes later Lyon Tucker came out and pumped my hand.

"Let me show you around," he said. He gave me the grand tour of the two studios, filled with modern TV equipment: Phillips color cameras and two RCA high band color recorders. I don't know what these gadgets are or what they do, but Tucker pointed to them with considerable pride and dropped their names as if he were strewing gold nuggets in my path.

We ended up in front of a broad picture window and looked across two miles of water at the lighthouse outside the harbor.

"How come you use that for a transmitter?" I asked. "You're higher up here."

"My first engineer developed the idea," he told me. "You see, we don't want to spill over into Boston, but we do want to reach up and down the coast. So we use a selective beam for the inland area, and an omnidirectional ground plane effect for the coastal zone. The water acts as a beam reflector."

"Oh," I said. What would *you* have answered?

Tucker switched on a TV monitor. The sound came on first, then the color picture. An announcer in a light blue suit said, "This lawlessness must stop. There are two factions in our community who keep the turmoil at fever pitch. They are the right-wing American Defenders and the militant youth element, the Body and Soul. These factions are on a collision course—and the result will be bloody warfare in the quiet streets of Pilgrim's Pride." He paused, and a white band of lettering, "A Channel Nine Editorial," appeared over his chest. He continued, "We urge immediate relaxation of the tension. For the public interest, both sides must be prepared to ease up a little in their demands. And soon. There is no time for delay." He put down his notes, gave us a serious look, and another voice came in and told us this had been a Channel Nine Editorial, and responsible parties for opposing viewpoints might request time to rebut it.

"How very generous of you, Father."

The high-pitched voice came from behind us. I swung around and saw Leslie Tucker, dressed in silky-looking pastel clothes, including a ruffly neck scarf.

"Hello, Leslie," Tucker said quietly. He was probably trying to make amends for the last conversation he'd had with his stepson. "Is this a social call?"

Leslie made a face. "Hardly. Business. We both know that Grandfather Garret had a fair-sized block of Tucker Enterprises stock, along with a directorship. I happen to know that his and Grandmother's wills give a goodly share of that stock to me. I intend to sell that stock on the open market as soon as their wills have been probated." His hand made a fluttery motion. "Perhaps it is indelicate of me to bring it up at this time. But I wanted you to know." Leslie smiled. "Out of fairness, if you know what I mean."

"Of course, Leslie," Tucker said curtly. "I understand you came to me out of fairness. But I'm afraid I have sad news for you. Whichever clerk in the lawyer's office you paid for your information about the wills didn't give you the whole story. There's a special proviso in the granting of those stock certificates giving the corporation first option to repurchase a decedent's shares over an extended period that won't work a financial hardship on the firm. I believe the time limit is ten years. So I'm afraid all you'll get is a nice little income, perhaps enough to carry the payments on a sports car. But congratulations anyway."

Leslie looked as if he had choked on his Adam's apple. "You—you—"

"Was there anything else, Leslie?" Lyon asked.

The boy turned on his heel and walked out. I tried to think of something to say, but just then the telephone on Tucker's desk rang.

"That will be Sam Bramin," he sighed, "demanding his equal TV time." He picked up the receiver. "Yes?" He looked puzzled as he handed me the receiver. "It's Charity. What's she doing at the police station?"

I shrugged, and took the phone. "This is Ben."

Her voice was excited. "I found something. It was buried in one of the witnesses' reports. Old Ham Perkins."

"Who's Old Ham Perkins?"

"Never mind, I'll tell you when you get there."

"Where's there?"

"Far side of the harbor from you. Take the Harbor Drive and follow it all the way out to the point.

61

There's an old lobster wharf—an exact copy of Motif Number One up in Rockport. You know, the one that's been in so many paintings."

"I'll find it," I said. "Twenty minutes."

As I hung up, I noticed that Lyon Tucker was glaring at me.

"Are you meddling in this after all, Shock?"

"Not meddling," I said. "I just think there are a few details that need looking into."

"I told you not to," he said. Before I could answer, the door opened and Scarlett came in. She stood silently, one hand on her outswung hip, that damned metal zipper glaring at me.

"I know you did," I said. "But sometimes there's a duty to the law that goes beyond personal wishes."

"You're an outsider. You have no stake in this."

"Charity's my stake."

"I warn you, Shock," he said. "Meddle any more and I'll have you jailed. I can do it."

I was getting a little sick of people threatening me today. "Don't throw your weight around, Mr. Tucker. I'm a big boy, too. And I know some cop tricks your Chief Cooke probably never heard of."

I started for the door. For a second it looked as if Scarlett wasn't going to move aside for me. Then she did, and as I passed her she smiled and whispered, "Bastard!"

SEVEN

I broke a few of Miles Cooke's precious rules as I moved the big Fleetwood through Pilgrim's Pride twenty miles an hour faster than the posted limit of 25.

Lyon Tucker's reaction had surprised me. It was excessive. I realized the man was under considerable strain, but even so, I suspected that he rarely made statements he wasn't prepared to back up. I hoped I was wrong. The last thing I needed was a battle with Charity's father.

I passed the town limits and after cruising along the water's edge for a half mile, I saw a red, barnlike building, perched on stilts, jutting out into the harbor.

Lobster traps were piled to one side of the building, and the smell of shellfish was ripe in the air. I went inside. Long wooden vats like horse troughs filled with sea water and dejected lobsters ran along the walls.

I walked past the lobster pens and out onto the pier on the harbor side of the building, and found Charity talking with a weather-beaten old man who looked like Wallace Beery. He wore high-bibbed overalls, and a corncob pipe was stuck between his white-whiskered jaws.

"Ben," Charity said, "this is Ham Perkins."

"Ayeh," said Ham Perkins. I pumped his hand.

"Ham saw the explosion," Charity told me.

The old man pointed at a place midway between the headland of the opposite side of the harbor and the outskirts of Pilgrim's Pride.

"There was a flash right 'bout there," he said. "Then somethin' whooshed' cross the water like a skyrocket and Mr. Tucker's boat went down like she'd been torpedoed."

"Have you got any field glasses?" I asked.

"Got somethin' better'n that," he said. He went inside for a moment and reappeared with a long brass telescope. I tried to train it on the opposite shore, but the beating of my heart bounced it around too much. I rested it on top of one of the posts and swept it along the water's edge. I found few buildings in the area he had indicated. The only ones of any size at all were another pier and some sheds behind it.

I steadied the telescope on the pier and asked Perkins to take a look. "Ayeh," he said, "it was just 'round there."

"What's the matter with Cooke?" I said. "Ham has pinpointed the firing site and Cooke wrote it down without understanding what he missed."

"You missed it too, Ben," Charity said sweetly. "Not that I blame you. What Ham told the officer was that he'd seen the explosion and a flash like summer lightning. Everybody took that to mean they were the same flash. Actually, one came before the other."

"Everybody's in too much of a hurry these days," the old codger said. "I could tell they weren't interested in anythin' I had to say. They took it down and went 'bout their business. I knew the Garrets. Nice people. They bought from me regular. If I can help out any way, you just let me know."

"I'll do that," I promised. Charity and I got back in the car and I began my hourly run through Pilgrim's Pride. By now the Fleetwood practically knew its own way.

"Are you going to tell Chief Cooke about this?" Charity asked.

I gave her a quick look. "Didn't *you?*"

She shook her head. "I wanted to talk with Ham

first. I could have been wrong, you know. But there was something about that summer lightning remark that caught my eye."

We made several false starts trying to get to the waterfront. Most of the roads led to private homes. Then we lucked in.

I looked at the fence around a long pier and some adjoining buildings and said, "Ho, ho, ho!"

A sign read, "No Trespassing. Property of S. Bramin."

"I don't feel right about this," Charity said as we got out of the car. "I think we ought to notify the Chief and let him take care of it."

"Leave it to Ben," I said. Yeah, big brawny Ben, with bravado where his brains should be. "You just wait in the car."

"Oh, no," she said, slipping out her mini-camera. "You forget who ferreted out this place."

I should have stopped her right then. One tight squeeze a day was more than enough for a girl who was running on sheer nerve to begin with. But there was a selfish gratification in having her along to watch me operate at my best.

Using a set of spring-steel picks I carry on my key ring, I had no trouble opening the rusty padlock on the gate.

It was just after one in the afternoon by the sweep hand of my diving watch as we slipped around the edge of the building nearest the pier.

The area of the harbor where *Channel Nine* had gone down was directly ahead. It was like looking down a shooting gallery. The boat would have been an easy target for a recoilless rifle.

I snooped around searching for a mark, a blast burn—anything. A recoilless rifle is almost as danger-ous to those behind it as to those in front. When it goes off, it shoots back a gust of flame that could roast a man alive. I looked for burn marks on the building. No luck.

"Ben!" Charity shrieked. "Look out!"

Something flapped against my face. I flailed my arms and jumped back in surprise.

A big, gray owl was attacking me. It fluttered around some more, out of its element in the bright sunlight, then flew up and disappeared into the shadows under the eaves of the building.

Charity let out a sigh. I held her gently by both shoulders.

"It's going to be all right, baby," I said. "Relax."

She leaned her head against my chest. I felt big and protective, guarding her against the evils of the world.

Just then I heard a metallic click—a pistol's hammer being cocked. I stiffened. Charity started to turn. In a low voice, I warned, Don't move."

"Good idea, boss," said a deep voice. "Just keep your mitts on the lady's bazoom." A hand fumbled inside my jacket and lifted out my .38. I heard footsteps moving slowly away from us, and then the voice said, "Okay, turn around. Slow."

EIGHT

I turned around very slowly indeed.

He was a typical bully-boy: heavy, with a thick black belt that cut deeply into his gut, vanishing under the folds of fat. His pudgy fist clutched a .45 service automatic. The experts say it can knock a man down if the bullet touches his little finger. The size of the barrel pointing at me tended to confirm that claim.

Behind him, in the nearest building, a door opened. Sam Bramin emerged, dressed in a light-colored summer suit. He looked as if he were on his way to deliver ice cream.

"Why, look here," he said. "It's Miss Charity and Mr. Shock from the City. Bruno, treat this gentleman with respect. He's a police officer."

"Big deal," Bruno grumbled.

"Bruno Wessel, one of my assistants," Sam Bramin said. "Bruno, why don't you keep Miss Tucker company while Mr. Shock and I have a brief discussion."

"We must have lost our way," I suggested. It didn't work. Bruno Wessel gave us a decaying grin and beckoned Charity over to a shaded part of the pier. Sam Bramin threw me an "I'm waiting" look, and I figured, what the hell—maybe when I got him alone, away from Bruno, I might be able to work something out. I followed him into the building.

His office was anything but ornate. A beat-up old desk and a couple of chairs were the only furnishings. There wasn't any air conditioning, and I could feel the sweat pouring down my back.

Sam Bramin leaned back in his swivel chair with that special awkwardness I've noticed about fat people, as if somewhere under all that blubber there's a skinny guy wearing a fat-man suit he hasn't quite gotten used to.

"This is a delicate situation, Mr. Shock," he began. "On the one hand, I don't want any trouble—especially with a representative of the New York Police Department."

"Off duty," I reminded him. He rewarded me with a big grin.

"And trespassing," he added. "On private property."

"We were looking for the road to Rockport," I said.

He shook his head. "Sorry, Mr. Shock. We watched you open the gate lock. Very efficient. You obviously have a good deal of practice."

I waited to see what he was driving at.

"Don't you think I am entitled to a bit of curiosity?" he asked. "Am I not entitled to ask, what is this man doing prowling around my private property? The fact that he is an off-duty policeman only increases my curiosity. Because I then ask myself—is he really off duty? Or is he on some assignment? Can you see the quandary I find myself in, Mr. Shock?"

I didn't answer. Instead, I threw a wild card on the table: "Just how rough were your business dealings with Lyon Tucker?"

"That happened a long time ago," he said. Bingo! "They were ordinary business transactions with nothing to distinguish them."

"Except that you got outsharped," I said. I figured Lyon Tucker couldn't have ended up owning half of Pilgrim's Pride by being Mr. Nice Guy.

My hunch was right. Bramin reacted as if I had whipped out a Soviet flag.

"Tucker was far from ethical," he said angrily.

68

"That was why I broke off my relationship with him. For a while, it appeared that we might form one of the most successful real estate firms in New England. But while your friend Mr. Tucker is a stickler for the letter of a contract, he is always quick to take advantage of any loopholes."

Nasty Mr. Tucker, I thought. I wondered how many loopholes Sam Bramin had explored in his day.

"I made no accusations," Bramin continued. "I presumed the parting was amicable. But Lyon took it harder than I did."

"And he started dumping on the American Defenders?"

"Fiercely. And most unfairly. Oh, he was obliged to provide equal time for me to answer his allegations—and I took advantage of it. But he has constantly tried to keep me on the defensive."

I wondered where all this was leading.

He didn't keep me waiting. "I have had occasion to—ah—look into your career," he said. "You are obviously a very skilled police officer. But, if you will forgive me, your reputation leaves something to be desired. "

"You must have been burning up the phone wires."

He shrugged. "Information is a basic commodity in my business. And if my information is correct, your career is somewhat under a cloud just now."

"So what?"

"Perhaps it's fortunate that you paid me this visit," he said. "I have an inkling of what is behind it. You think I had something to do with the—unfortunate accident."

"You said it, not me."

"I said it," he came back, "because I am innocent of such charges and so I dare to speak them aloud. It was totally unnecessary for you to practice your lockpicking arts on me, Mr. Shock. Had you called, permission to inspect these premises would have been given to you instantly."

"I'm sorry I didn't know that. Look, what's on your mind, Mr. Bramin? I know I'm technically guilty of trespassing, but that's not why you're bending my ear. Why don't you get to the point?"

"Very well," he said, squinching his rotund form around in the creaking chair. "I take it you're familiar with the work of the American Defenders?"

"Familiar enough."

"We represent the front line of American patriots fighting against the corruption of our nation. We stand shoulder to shoulder against the infiltration of foreign doctrines into our study of American heritage. We are real Americans."

"The only real American are the Indians," I said. It didn't even register.

"Many of our positions are unpopular," he went on, like a tape recorder. "The so-called liberals attack our position on the question of young militants. Good Lord, Mr. Shock, we aren't anti-youth. Even some of the young people are recognizing this today. As for the rest—those who call the Defenders anti-youth—they are at best misguided idealists."

"Is the Mayor of New York a misguided idealist?" I asked. The Mayor had publically blasted the Defenders on the occasion of their visit to the City.

"That poor man." Bramin smiled condescendingly. "He inherited a tainted city and there isn't anything one man could do to correct its flaws. He has a majority of Jews and blacks and limousine liberals, and naturally he has to appeal to them to remain in office."

"Bramin," I said, fed up, "I hope you take this personally. As far as I'm concerned, you're an idiot."

His smile vanished. "Then you won't consider joining our organization?"

"I'd sooner join the Nazi Party."

He took it badly. He wrenched himself out of the chair, anger twisting his flaccid face.

"You—" he sputtered, "Mr. Shock, you are a very shortsighted man!"

"I'll have my eyes examined," I promised. He appeared ready to go into a fit of some kind. I don't know what would have happened next if Charity hadn't screamed.

I was halfway through the door before her voice stopped ringing in my ears. The scream was familiar, the way the taste of blood is instantly recognizable when you bite your tongue. It was the same scream I had heard months before as she collapsed under the rapist.

When I burst out into the blazing sunlight, it was like a nightmare repeated.

Charity was huddled back against an overturned boat hull. Bruno Wessel was moving in on her, his gun tucked away in his hip pocket and his fly gaping open.

"Bruno!" Sam Bramin called.

Wessel looked around. By then I was alongside him and I gave him a zinging right to the gut. My fist sank in almost to the wrist and he heaved a *whoomphing* sigh, fell to his knees, and started puking on the sun-dappled ground.

"That wasn't necessary, Mr. Shock," said Sam Bramin.

"Shove it!" I yelled. I grabbed Charity and pulled her up against my chest. The heat had caused her shirt to stick wetly to her back. She tried to get away from me, fear distorting her face.

"A Mexican stand-off," said Bramin. "You were

71

wrong in trespassing, and Bruno was wrong in believing this young lady invited his—ah—advances. Suppose we just call it a draw?"

"I wouldn't make a deal with you if you offered me a signed guarantee from J. Edgar Hoover."

"Don't be rash," he said.

"Get the hell out of my way," I said. By then Wessel had rolled over on his stomach, groaning. I took my gun from his belt, then yanked the .45 from his hip pocket and heaved it into the harbor.

"I can get you in trouble," Bramin warned.

"Go ahead," I said. "How much trouble do you think *you're* in? How many guys in town have a seventy-five-millimeter recoilless rifle?"

"None here!" he bellowed. "No such thing! Lies, lies are the weapons our enemies use against us. Rifles, yes. Right of the citizen to bear arms. Constitutional! But a recoilless rifle? Never."

"Sure," I said, leading Charity from the fenced-in yard. Sam Bramin looked after us as we got into the Fleetwood. Bruno Wessel sat clutching his gut.

We drove away. "I'm sorry about that, baby," I said to Charity. "That bastard inside was batting his gums and I was listening, hoping he'd deliver something I could use. I didn't have any idea what was happening outside."

"It's all right, Ben. I suppose I'm getting used to being raped."

Her voice was dead and toneless. I gave her a quick look. She was staring straight ahead. A thin shimmer of sweat beaded her upper lip.

"Charity," I said helplessly.

"Perhaps you shouldn't have stopped him," she said. "I might have enjoyed it."

I cursed under my breath. She ignored me. Out-

72

wardly, she seemed calm enough. I'd have been less worried if she wasn't.

At the first Shell station I stopped to telephone Miles Cooke.

"I need a good doctor fast," I told him.

"Gunshot?" he asked.

"Aggravated mental shock. Charity."

"Head over this way. I'll pick you up outside the police station and lead you to a good man. I'll call ahead."

When we came in sight of the main part of town he was waiting in his souped-up Merc. He waved for me to follow him, and we broke every speed law on the books on the way through Pilgrim's Pride.

Dr. Robert Jordan lived two miles out of town, on the road to Rockport. On our way to his home we passed the lobster wharf. Ham Perkins was nowhere in sight.

When we parked in Jordan's driveway, Charity got out of the car slowly, as if she had intended to make this visit all along.

"I know Dr. Jordan very well," she told me. Her speech was noticeably slurred. "I interviewed him once for my father's television station."

"Sure you did, honey," I mumbled.

I thanked Cooke and told him I'd take it from there, that he didn't have to wait. He got back in his Merc and took off. A good man, that one.

Dr. Jordan was waiting, hypodermic needle in hand. He injected Charity with something colorless. She didn't seem to react to it.

"What happened?" he asked.

I told him. I also told him about the rape in New York.

He nodded. "I'm not surprised," he said. "It's just

too much. She has to go under, otherwise she'll come apart."

He held her left hand up in the air and then took his own away. She kept her hand up there until I couldn't stand it any more and reached over to lower it onto her lap.

"Is she in any danger?" I asked, feeling an aching void open up in my innards.

"Not really," he said. "It's just that everything has piled up on her. The thing in New York, then her grandparents, and now this. Which." he added, "Chief Cooke didn't seem to know anything about."

I smiled bleakly. "I don't see why Miles should know everything about everybody."

He smiled back. "I agree. I presume you're attending to the man responsible?"

"He's already been taken care of."

"I thought as much," he said, looking at my skinned knuckles. "I'll put some medication on those if you don't mind. It would be an affront to my professional standing if anyone developed blood poisoning after leaving my office."

I seemed to be meeting all the good ones in Pilgrim's Pride. I let him smear some ointment over my hand. All the while Charity sat there with a quiet smile on her face, as if she were listening to some distant music.

The front door opened and Lyon Tucker came barging in. He gave me a curt nod as he went over to his daughter.

"Miles called me," he said to Jordan. "What is it, Bob?"

Jordan said, "Reaction to the thing yesterday." His standing in my book went up by three thousand points.

"Are you sure that's all?" Tucker asked.

74

"That's all, Lyon."

"What does she need? Name it. Specialists? Get them in. Whatever you want."

Jordan shrugged. "She's a tired girl," he said. "A little R and R'll do it, I'd say."

"What the hell's R and R?"

Jordan looked in my direction. "Rest and recuperation," he said. "My guess is that Mr. Shock'll see to that. Don't worry yourself, Lyon. She's as strong as an ox."

"Don't kid me, Bob," said Tucker.

"Lyon," said the doctor slowly, "I wouldn't dream of kidding you. Now, you and Mr. Shock take her home and let her sleep about twenty hours and pour a few drinks down her if she wakes up. I give you my personal gold-plated guarantee: she'll be all right."

I took her arm. "Thanks, Doc."

She rose, zombie-like, and followed me out of the room.

"Keep an eye on her tonight," said Jordan. "There's a chance she might sleepwalk, although it's not likely."

"Send me your bill, Bob," said Tucker.

"When have I ever forgotten a bill?" said Jordan. "I'd rather take it out in TV advertising, but you know how the American Medical Association feels about that."

Charity got into Lyon's car, I crawled into mine, and we drove back into town.

The sun burned down on us. I began to feel a dull hatred for this sleepy little tourist town. It seemed to be glaring at me from its shadowed windows. All the way up the hill I glared back.

NINE

Tucker pulled the Continental off the road a few hundred yards below the house. I drew up behind him and we got out.

"Shock," he said, "I suggest we declare a truce. Both of us are concerned about Charity. That comes first. Right?"

He stuck out his hand. I took it and said, "Right."

"Now, about my wife, Bethesda."

"What about her?"

"She's had a lot to handle. Maybe we can just smuggle Charity into her bedroom. Without Bethesda knowing. Will you help?"

"I don't think it's such a good idea," I said. "Things like this have a way of spilling out."

"I don't want to upset Bethesda any more," he insisted.

"Okay," I said. "If I can help, I will. But I still think it's a mistake."

I got back in the Fleetwood and followed him up to the house. High above it I saw the widow's walk, empty in the bright sunlight. I shut off the engine and went up to help Charity out of the car. She was so quiet and sedate, so distant, that I wanted to call out: "Baby, I'm here! Look at me!" But I kept my yap shut. Lyon Tucker took her by the arm and we went into the house quietly, without ringing the bell.

Our stealth was a big waste of time.

Bethesda Tucker wheeled herself over to the sloping ramp and looked up at us.

"My poor baby," she said.

"Charity's tired," Tucker said softly.

"Tired!" cried his wife. "Poor thing, I know what's happened. Dr. Jordan called. Give her to me."

"Goddam Dr. Jordan!" said her husband.

"It's all right, darling," Bethesda said. "He was right to call. He's a sly boots, for a doctor. He's trying to cure two patients for the price of one. Let me have her, Lyon. It's all right. I'll take care of my baby."

Somehow you forgot that she was in a wheelchair. Charity held out her hand the way a little girl will reach out to hold her mother's fingertips—except that Charity towered over the slight, dark figure in the wheelchair. Together, they started to leave the room, Bethesda scudding along so deftly that you got the impression the chair was self-propelled.

Before they got to the door, it opened and in walked a figure right off an Army recruiting poster. He must have been six feet six; he stood ramrod straight, wearing the khaki of the U.S. Army and the eagles of a colonel.

"Oh, Matthew," said Bethesda, "this is Ben Shock. He's a good friend of Charity's."

"Matt Martin's the name," he said, putting out his hand. "I head up the local National Guard outfit."

His chestful of fruit salad made it clear that he had been to a few places besides Pilgrim's Pride. I spotted ribbons for Vietnam, Korea, and both the ETO and Pacific Theaters from World War II.

He noticed me giving his chest the once-over. "You look like you know what these are," he said.

"Some of them," I said. "Particularly the Combat Infantryman's Badge."

He touched the long rectangle with a rifle etched against a field of blue. "You were over there, too?" he asked.

"For a while," I said. We shook hands. Lyon Tucker made no move to join the festivities.

"Hello, Bull," he said. "What brings you over here?"

Colonel Martin said, "I naturally wanted to express my condolences about the accident. Chief Cooke told me about it."

"Any chance of you telling us why you were talking with Cooke?" I asked.

"No problem," said Martin. "After I heard about the explosion, I checked out our arsenal. There are two satchel charges missing. I suggested to Cooke that they might have been planted on the boat."

"That's confidential police information then," Tucker said angrily. "You shouldn't be spouting it off in front of anyone who comes along."

Martin looked puzzled. "Sorry, Lyon."

"Damn you," said Tucker, "don't call me Lyon." He barged out of the room. Bethesda and Charity followed him.

"What was all that about?" I asked.

Martin sighed. "Lyon and I have known each other for a long time. Let it go at that."

"No sir," I insisted. "I think you ought to explain the trouble between you two."

The Colonel headed for the sideboard as if he knew where he was going and splashed some burbon into a glass. "Have one?" he asked me.

It wasn't mid-afternoon yet—but I'd been through enough today to make up for a week on duty. "Scotch," I said, "and don't worry about the lubber line."

He took me at my word and dumped a good three ounces of Dewar's White Label into a glass over a couple of ice cubes that were so cold they squeaked when the liquor covered them.

"I've known Bethesda for a long while," Martin said, sipping at his drink. "Out in California. Long

78

before Lyon met her, as a matter of fact. You may not know this, but his first wife, Mary—Charity's mother— was from California, too. She and Bethesda were close friends. I put in a couple of long tours at Camp Stoneman and I knew both Mary and Bethesda."

He stared out the window, down toward the sea. "We all suspected there was something more than neighborly friendship between Bethesda and Lyon. And, of course, we were proved right when he married her less than two years after Mary died."

He had made a second drink and was pouring it down at a fast clip.

"I was overseas when Mary died," he said slowly. "I always liked her. She and Bethesda were such good friends. I was never engaged to Bethesda, but I felt there was an understanding between us. Then, while I was on Okinawa, good old Lyon offered her his home and hearth, and there you go."

I didn't say anything. It was obvious that the colonel was a little drunk.

"I never lost my feeling for Bethesda," he said. "Nor did I ever forget that she was once an active, gloriously healthy, woman, before that drunken bastard made a mistake in cinching her saddle. It slipped, she fell, and . . ."

He dumped the remains of his drink down, made a move toward the bourbon bottle, and reconsidered. He put the glass down on the table and examined it as if it were an enemy mortar.

"That was a long time ago," I said.

"Hate endures," he told me. Then he repeated it: "Hate endures. First Lyon took her away from me, then he crippled her."

I stared at him. This was a man who obviously hated Lyon Tucker. But how much? Enough to murder him?

"Listen," I said, "can I talk with whoever's in charge of your explosives and heavy weapons?"

Bull Martin waved his hand vaguely. "No sweat. Drop over any time. Ask for Ordnance Sergeant Bruno Wessel."

I made him repeat it.

"Wessel," he mumbled. "Big fat guy. Can't miss him. Tell him I said it's all right to give you details. Be glad to help."

I bet Wessel would. The whole business was becoming, as Alice said about Wonderland, "curiouser and curiouser."

TEN

I decided to pay Bramin's pier a return visit. But there were things to attend to first. I had to be sure Charity was all right.

She was sleeping, a sad little smile on her face. Bethesda sat in her wheelchair next to Charity's bed.

"Come in, Mr. Shock," she said.

"Call me Ben, please," I said.

"Thank you," she replied.

I sat down on a padded window seat. Far down the hill I could see the violent blue of the ocean.

The room looked as if a little girl still lived in it. The curtains were painted with pictures of Winnie the Pooh, and Alice chased the White Rabbit around the fringes of the lamp shade.

Bethesda's voice brought me back. "You love her, don't you, Ben?"

"Yes ma'am," I said. "It looks that way."

"That—mess in the city. It hurt her very badly."

"I know."

"Ben," she said hesitantly. "You'll stay around, won't you? Until after the funeral tomorrow, at least?"

"I'll stay as long as she needs me," I said.

We sat without talking. Both of us stared at Charity and sank into our own private thoughts.

This was the nitty-gritty. When you're out there on the street protecting a nameless and faceless Society from evil-doers it becomes simply a professional task. Hands up, sir—nothing personal, of course.

But when they come after you own, the game changes. That's when you forgot all that nice stuff

81

about the rights of the accused, about being innocent until proven guilty. That's when characters like Bruno Wessel had better watch where they walk, because it would be very easy for them to come down with a bad case of broken ribs.

My father was one of the last of the old-style cops. He felt that whenever he had to make an arrest he had failed somewhere earlier. In his world, the cop on the beat bent a few heads to show the kids the folly of stealing hub caps and—true enough—that made him both judge and jury. But when the lumps went down, the kids were left with a headache and an increased respect for the instant might of the Law. They didn't have rap sheets that would follow them the rest of their lives.

I wondered what Pop would have done with Bruno this morning. Probably exactly what I did. That made me feel a little better.

My chin bounced against my chest. I got up and stretched. Bethesda was asleep in her wheelchair. Charity had turned over, now the gentle smile was gone and there was a little frown furrowing a deep line between her brow. I stroked her forehead and the frown softened. I bent down and brushed a kiss against her moist cheek. She murmured something and I said, "It's all right, baby."

Out in the hall, I turned the wrong way. It led to stairs that I climbed and found myself on the widow's walk.

The view was spectacular. The ocean spread out below. Any clipper ship climbing over the horizon in the old days must have been visible half a day out.

Someone else was enjoying the view. Leslie turned and glowered at me.

"So you're still here," he said.

"I don't know what's eating you," I said. "But don't

show me your teeth or I'll push them down your throat."

"Don't threaten me, you bully!" he said.

I didn't feel particularly proud of myself. First Scarlett, now her brother. Go to it, Ben old boy. Beat up the school kids while you're at it.

"Listen," I said, "this has been a lousy two days. Everybody's tensed up. Forget what I said."

"Why don't you go back to New York?" he said. "You aren't wanted here."

I sighed. Hold up an olive branch and they stick you in the eye with it.

He clutched something against his side, hiding it from me with his body. I stepped around him and saw a set of high-powered binoculars.

"Nice glasses," I said, reaching for them. He jerked them away as if my hand would contaminate their shiny black leather.

"Stay away from me!" he snapped, and scuttled backward, off the widow's walk and down the stairs. He started to run and almost tripped over his own feet. I had really spooked the kid. I wondered why.

I didn't need binoculars to see that the Bramin pier was in plain view from here. There wasn't any activity visible to my naked eye. So far as I could see, there wasn't a soul stirring in Pilgrim's Pride.

It was tempting to stand there and enjoy the view, but I had work to do. I wanted to have another look around Bramin's storage depot. It was just too much of a coincidence that Bruno Wessel should be Bramin's chief henchman and also be the local National Guard's ordnance sergeant. Certainly Miles Cooke must have known this. I wondered why he hadn't seen fit to mention it to me.

I went down the stairs quickly. As I neared the first landing my feet went out from under me and only a quick grab at the railing kept me from tumbling tail over teacup. A handful of marbles cascaded against the wall.

My behind ached where it had whacked into the lip of one of the stairs. I picked up a couple of the marbles. Just ordinary everyday glassies, twenty-five for a quarter. I suspected Leslie's delicate hand in strewing them on the stairs. I could almost hear him laughing like hell if I had limped downstairs with a broken leg. I gathered up the marbles—twelve in all—to keep someone else from busting their ass, and dropped them in the umbrella rack in the main hallway. They sounded like the pinball machine to end all pinball machines as they clattered their way down among the bumbershoots.

The Fleetwood awaited, wearing its cobwebbed battle scars. The sun had heated up the leather seat, and my behind started aching again as I let the car coast down the hill in low.

As I cruised into Pilgrim's Pride, the bell in the picture-postcard church steeple tolled five. I checked my Nivada Grenchen Sea Diver. It read 5:02. That meant the church steeple was two minutes slow. The Nivada was adjusted to a loss or gain of two seconds a week. Providing I remembered to wind it.

There seemed to be some excitement in the town square. In fact, the streets were blocked with people. I pulled over to the curb, sliding deftly into place in front of a parking meter that still had more than a good half an hour of time indicated on its flag. A nickel here, a nickel there . . .

Until then, I hadn't noticed all the Chambers of Commerce signs in the center of town, boosting the upcoming Fourth of July festivities.

"FOOD . . . MUSIC . . . FIREWORKS!" one blared in

red and blue letters. "ANNUAL PILGRIM'S PRIDE FOURTH OF JULY CELEBRATION AT TUCKER FIELD."

Tucker Field? Well, why not? Lyon Tucker owned practically everything else in town.

The sign didn't mention any speeches, but knowing politicians, I was willing to lay five to two that the audience wouldn't get off that easy.

As I moved through the crowd, I started to feel uneasy. This wasn't an ordinary gathering of civilians. For one thing, there wasn't a woman in sight. And almost every man I saw was wearing an armband with a white star on a blue field, a red lightning bolt slashing through it—the emblem of the American Defenders.

The men looked at me with curiosity but not hostility, so I kept rummaging my way toward the front line. Another sign came into view.

"OUTDOOR PAGEANT!" it read. "SEE THE EXCITING RE-ENACTMENT OF THE DEFENSE OF PILGRIM'S PRIDE AGAINST HOSTILE INDIANS BY CAPTAIN JOHN CROSS AND HIS GALLANT PILGRIMS. STARRING COLONEL MATTHEW MARTIN AS CAPTAIN JOHN CROSS."

That would be exciting for Bull Martin, I thought. From Korea and Vietnam to play-acting with phony Indians. I wondered who would play the Indians.

It seemed to me that Pilgrim's Pride had problems considerably more complicated than ancient Indian attacks. But boys will be boys.

"Testing, testing, one two three four," said a vaguely familiar voice, blasting through a set of outdoor loudspeakers. (If I ever go on the speaking circuit, I intend to check my P.A. equipment by saying, "I'm talking into this gadget to see if anybody can hear me.")

The voice counted up to four again. I came out of

85

the crowd and saw who was muttering into the mike.

My old buddy, Bruno Wessel.

He wore what seemed to be a combination of the uniforms of all three American armed services with a nasty touch of the Brown Shirts thrown in. He sported mirror-polished jump boots, and—so help me—a baby-blue beret!

I faded back into the crowd of American Defenders so he couldn't see me. I wanted to find out what was going on.

If it hadn't been so frightening, the scene would have been funny. With his bulging gut spilling out over his belt, Wessel was every inch the caricature of military excess. He was flanked by a pair of creased American flags that flapped listlessly in the late afternoon breeze.

While Wessel convinced himself that the P.A. really was working, I squinted around. There were less than a hundred men in the town square, and two-thirds of them wore the American Defenders' armband. That said something for the ordinary townspeople of Pilgrim's Pride; at least they weren't turning out in big numbers to provide Bramin's gang with an audience. Of course, by "not getting involved," they weren't doing anybody any good, either.

"Okay, men," shouted Wessel. "Looks like everybody who's coming is here." He peered around, counting the house. "I don't have time today to take a roll call, but you can pass the word that I will next time. Enough said. Now, some of you thought we should have had this meeting at our Center. You know what Commander Bramin said to that. The American Defenders stand for all pureblooded Americans. And some of the good people who are secretly on our side are not ready to commit themselves openly by paying a visit to the Center."

86

If the shabby pier and its raunchy shacks were the "Center," I didn't blame anybody for wanting to stay away—although I hadn't forgotten my own private plan to drop in unannounced again.

"Now," Wessel went on, "We've gotten a legal permit and we're out here in the light of day, everything above-board, to let the people of Pilgrim's Pride hear the truth once more. And the truth is this: we haven't got anything against minority groups. Whether they're Chinese or Jews or blacks or you-name-it."

There came a mutter from the crowd. I couldn't tell if it was one of assent or anger.

"Well," Wessel went on, "we sure ain't got any Chinese problem here in Pilgrim's Pride. And we ain't got any black or Jew problem. The few who live here stay out of the way, and as long as they keep their noses clean we aren't going to insist that they go back to Israel or Africa or China."

Good for you, Bruno.

"It's the hippies who are stirring up a mess. We've tried to live and let live, but those dirty long-haired Commies over in Shame Town are stockpiling weapons and dope and God-knows-what, and planning a massacre that will have blood running in the streets if we let them pull it off!

"It isn't going to do any good to complain to the mayor," Wessel shouted. "It ain't going to do any good to go to the police. The mayor and the police have their hands tied by the Supreme Court and the sell-out artists in the state capital. No sir, men, it's up to us! We must be alert! We must be on guard! We must be . . . *Defenders!*"

It must have been a standard rallying cry, because suddenly the square echoed with a hundred voices crying, *"We are Defenders!"*

I suddenly realized I was wasting precious time.

87

If Wessel and most of his gang were here, the pier was probably wide open.

But before I had time to ease through the crowd a figure strolled casually out of an alley and jumped up onto the platform.

It was a long-haired man dressed in leather. From a distance he seemed to resemble the man I had encountered on the stage of the Bijou Theater, but I couldn't be sure.

In the stunned silence, his voice came over the microphone clearly and distinctly.

"If you don't mind, Sergeant Major," he said, "I'd like an opportunity to comment on several of your remarks." He lifted the microphone out of the surprised Wessel's fist.

"To begin with, many of us in Shame Town have as much or more love for our country than you Defenders. It's because we do love our country that we can't accept the disgraceful things certain men in government are forcing her to do. Now, you cats think it was swell that your immigrant forefathers drove the Indians off their own land, and every year you get up a big festival to celebrate it. Brothers, I'm here today to tell you *this* Fourth of July, the Indians might be the good guys, and old John Cross is going to have to watch his scalp or it might get lifted by a Body and Soul tomahawk!"

Wessel reacted first. "Defenders!" he yelled. "Get him!"

The crowd roared and started toward the platform. Then a smoking bottle arched down from one of the nearby buildings and splashed against the platform, bursting into orange flames. As the crowd hesitated, the long-haired man stepped deftly down, seemed to vanish into the flames, and was gone.

"Get the bastard!" Wessel screamed.

His followers started toward the alley and were met with a hail of bricks and bottles thrown down the roofs.

Shouting and cursing, the Defenders spread out. Meanwhile, the bell in the church steeple began to toll rapidly and I had a vision of dozens of volunteer firemen dropping their first before-dinner drinks and sprinting for the firehouse.

I got back into the Fleetwood, made a U-turn, and took off. Two blocks away, I passed a red fire engine headed for the town square, its siren screaming. It was followed, at top speed, by Miles Cooke in his souped-up Merc.

Poor Miles. When he pinned that star onto his shirt he latched onto one hot chunk of metal.

I took a roundabout way to the Bramin pier. I found a little stand of scrub trees a hundred yards away, eased the Fleetwood into them, and headed for the fence.

I checked quickly to make sure it wasn't electrified or gimmicked with some kind of burglar alarm. There didn't seem to be anything hooked up, so I shinnied up a post and dropped neatly on the other side, breathing a little harder than I used to when I learned the same trick in the Marines. Of course, now I lugged around an extra twenty pounds, which didn't help any either.

I checked out the buildings, one by one. There didn't seem to be anyone around. Then I tried the doors. They were all locked. My set of picks took care of that. I crept inside like the burglar I was and started looking.

The first building netted only a huge paper-baling machine which apparently shredded old posters and newspapers into neat, compact rectangles about the size of a bale of hay. I ran my hand along its side.

It was warm. It had been in use not too long ago. But, except for several tall stacks of Sam Bramin's *The American Way*, his manifesto for national reform, there wasn't anything else to see. Four huge bales of the books had obviously been put through the machine and were waiting to be carted off for salvage.

I went through the other four buildings, saving the office in which we'd talked for last.

It was the only one that paid off. The others had contained cabinets and boxes of records; this one four crates of concussion grenades, two of tear gas, fifty M-16 rifles.

I made a mental bet that if Bull Martin checked his small-arms stocks at the armory, he might come up a little short.

A cardboard box under the desk contained nine .45 caliber automatics and a couple of dozen empty clips. Nowhere in the building was there ammo for the weapons. I guessed that, as the really illegal part of the operation, it was safely stashed underground somewhere else.

As I rummaged around carefully in the waning light that sifted through the window, a scuffling noise came from behind the crates. I made a quick move for my .38.

"Okay, come out," I said. I couldn't imagine how I'd missed seeing one of the Defender rats during my search, but I wasn't taking any chances.

The rat came out.

He was a genuine, all-American, four-legged one, complete with whiskers and a long, hairy tail.

My heart started working again.

"Okay, Charlie," I said "Sorry. I didn't mean to insult you."

Charlie twitched his nose at me and scurried back into his hole.

I slipped out the door. The sun had long since set behind the hills to the west. The water in the harbor was now black and murky, except where it reflected the orange of a distant light.

I squatted on the edge of the pier, scowling. Unless Ham Perkins had been seeing things, the recoilless rifle *had* to have been fired from here.

But where was the evidence?

Just then the gray owl arrived again. This time he wasn't alone. There was a whole gang of them, what they call a parliament of owls. They fluttered around my face, beating at me with their wings.

"Knock it off!" I yelled. "I'm not a mouse. Go hoot at someone else."

Talk wasn't working, so I gave one of the birds a slam with the back of my hand. Feathers flew and he fled, jabbering, to the dark shadow under the building's eaves. His buddies followed him.

My curiosity was up. What the hell were a bunch of owls doing flapping down from their perches in daylight?

I found an oil drum to stand on and pulled myself up into the coolness under the eaves.

My nose smelled it out before I saw it.

No wonder my feathered friends were mad. One of their own was lying on the roof beam, roasted to a crisp. Still clutched in one talon was the wrinkled gray carcass of a field mouse.

I didn't need a road map. Friend owl had been returning from gathering breakfast and flew right into the backblast of a 75-mm recoilless rifle. In the same fiery breath, it knocked him under the eaves and into Eternity. And now his friends were mad at the world, for which I didn't blame them.

Taking the roasted owl by one foot, I shinnied down and tossed the smelly carcass into the harbor.

It made a *bloop* sound. I had a thought. Now if you had tossed a 75 in there. . . .

I called myself several kinds of idiot and headed for the car. This time, I used the gate. In fact, I could have done the same coming in because the lock was missing, and the gate was wide open.

I got the SCUBA gear out of the trunk and stripped down to my skivvies. This was getting to be an old act.

Flippers over one wrist, I padded back to the pier and slipped into the tank harness. My powerful underwater light pointed the way to a ladder descending into the water. I went down it slowly and winced when the icy water nipped at my toes. The harbor hadn't warmed up any since yesterday morning. I blew out the regulator and submerged.

It was easy to follow one of the pilings down to the sea floor. The water was surprisingly clear. But then, I wasn't in the East River.

The bottom was sandy, with rocks and some kelp. My light made a fuzzy circle as I swam back and forth in semicircular passes.

On the third one I found the 75.

It lay on the sand, half buried by the swirl of the tide. A light line was tied to the trigger housing. I followed the line and discovered that it was fastened loosely around one of the pier pilings.

Someone had tossed the weapon into the drink, confident that it wouldn't be rolled away by the tide.

I went back to the 75 and examined it carefully without touching it. Whoever hauled it up again was going to have to do some fast work to keep the salt water from rusting it out.

A little alarm bell was sounding inside my head. The damned thing was just too obvious, lying there on display, as if it were designed to entice the first skin diver who happened to come swimming by.

I decided not to disturb the merchandise, and swam up to the surface again.

The warm evening air was delightful against my goosebumps. I went inside and used the phone on Sam Bramin's desk to call Miles Cooke. Then I retrieved my clothes, dried down with an old blanket I use to wrap around the air tank, and sat down to wait.

ELEVEN

Every time I added it up, the total came out the same: somebody was trying to frame Sam Bramin. I didn't like this answer. I didn't like the bastard, and I ached to pin the twin murder rap on him. Uncoplike, maybe, but as I was saying, when they start coming after your own people, the beast in you surfaces.

Bramin wouldn't plant a frame on himself. Or would he? Could he have reasoned that such an obvious plant might divert suspicion from him?

A crunch of gravel announced the arrival of Cooke's Merc. I went out and blinked into the glare of its headlights. I could hear voices coming from inside the car. They were arguing.

I waited a while and then said loudly, "Okay, Chief, if you want everybody in town to know you're out here snooping, this is the way to do it."

The lights went out and three shadowy figures climbed out of the car. My eyes had been temporarily blinded by the direct beam of the headlights, and it was only when we got inside the shack that I was able to pick Cooke out of the group.

With him were two men I'd never seen before. The younger one wore the snappy uniform of a state trooper. The other was in civvies, but he had "cop" written all over him. He was a big, beefy guy who might have been fashioned out of old boilerplate and pile drivers.

"Ben Shock," Miles Cooke said, "Trooper Hailey and Detective Henry Koos. Shock's on the Force in New York City," he explained to Koos.

"I don't care if he's governor," Koos shot back. "He's out of his territory here. He's got no business interfering with an investigation and tampering with evidence."

"I haven't tampered with anything, Sergeant Koos," I said quickly.

"*Lieutenant*," he growled. Now I'd done it: demoted a man who obviously felt the full weight of his importance.

"Sorry," I said. "Anyway, Lieutenant, I haven't tampered with anything. The seventy-five is still down there on the bottom. I didn't touch it."

"Huh," he grunted and brushed past me, giving the shack the once-over. Cooke looked at me and shrugged apologetically.

"Lieutenant Koos is with the State Police," he said. "He's one of their top men in homicide. We're lucky to have him."

His voice sounded as if he had just announced he was lucky to have bubonic plague.

"Pleased to meet you, sir," said the young trooper, sticking out his hand. "How deep would you say the water is?"

"Fifteen feet," I said. I indicated my gear, dripping on the desk. "I used a lung. You're welcome—"

He grinned, climbing out of his uniform pants. "Never touch the stuff," he said. "I'd like to borrow your mask, flippers, and light, though."

"Be my guest," I said. By now he was down to his brightly colored boxer shorts. He had a deep tan all over and looked as if he would have been right at home hanging ten off a surfboard on some monster wave. We followed him out onto the pier. Inside, I could hear Koos rummaging around.

"It must be a big thrill to have the State Police's top homicide man helping out," I muttered to Cooke.

He cursed under his breath. "I couldn't help it," he said. "Sam Bramin pulled some strings and got him assigned to the case."

"Sam Bramin?" I said "How did *he* get into the act?"

"Search me," Cooke said. He started to say something else and then shut up so fast that I knew Koos was behind us.

"I hope you can explain your presence out here," Koos said to me. "This pier is private property."

"The bottom of the harbor isn't."

"You didn't drive your car along the bottom of the harbor."

"I didn't drive it onto private property, either. Listen, Koos, I don't know why you're making such a stink. It seems to me the real thing here is to find out who blasted two nice old people out of the water. And the murder weapon happens to be tied to this pier with a length of line."

"Which you could have tied yourself before calling us."

"Oh, my, my, my," said Miles Cooke. "Lieutenant Koos, please. Shock may have bent the rules a little, but it worked out for the best. Why don't we leave it there?"

"We'll see," Koos said. He glared at the trooper. "Well? What are you waiting for? It isn't going to swim up and wave at you."

Trooper Hailey paid no attention to him. He was sitting on the edge of the pier, breathing very deeply. I knew that he was hyperventilating himself—freeing his blood of carbon dioxide—to increase his time below. When he was ready, he held the mask against his face with one hand and the underwater light in the other, slipped off the pier, and went under with hardly a splash.

None of us said anything. When a man is under, your eyes are drawn to the spot where he was last seen. The harbor water looked black and greasy. Seconds dragged by. Once or twice there was a murky glimmer of the light beneath the surface. Then a minute passed without even that.

"He's been down there an awful long time," Koos said, breaking the silence.

"He knows what he's doing," I said. "By the look of the chest on him I bet he could stay down three minutes without worrying."

Koos gave me a dirty look and said nothing. It was obvious we were going to be great friends.

So much more time passed that now even I began to get concerned. The water was so cold that the trooper might have had a sudden cramp double him up, helpless, fifteen feet below the surface. But if that had happened, we should have seen the bubbles as he gasped for breath.

Then we heard a sound like a whale surfacing. The beam of a light probed in our direction.

"It's down there all right," Hailey's voice called. "Should I bring it up?"

Cooke hesitated and Koos leaped into the breech. "Hell, yes. Get it up here so we can see if it's what this guy says it is."

"Hold on," I said. "Look, there's no way we could positively link this weapon to the round that was fired into *Channel Nine*. It might have been this seventy-five; it might have been half a dozen others. But what seems clear to me is that they weren't trying to get rid of it, therefore the line. All they'd have to do is drag a light grapple along the end of the pier, snag the line, and haul the thing up."

"Make up your minds," called Hailey. "It's colder than blue blazes down here."

Koos opened his mouth but I cut him off. "*Or,*" I went on, "maybe somebody's trying to frame Sam Bramin. Maybe they wanted us to find the weapon and think somebody had stashed it there to drag up later."

"What do you have in mind?" Miles Cooke asked.

"Leave it down there. Sooner or later somebody's going to get itchy to find out if it's been discovered. Put a man someplace with a good pair of night glasses and get a make on whoever shows up."

"Are you through putting in your two cents' worth?" Koos asked.

"His two cents sounds pretty smart to me," said Cooke. "Come on in, Hailey. We're going to leave it down there."

"Okay," the trooper yelled. As he splashed his way toward us I could hear his teeth chattering.

Koos cursed. "This is your responsibility, Chief. My recommendation is that you pull that weapon out of there and examine it."

"You're right, Lieutenant," Cooke said. "It *is* my responsibility. And it's my decision to take Shock's suggestion. That seventy-five isn't going anywhere. I'd sure like to know who put it down there—especially if someone's trying to frame Sam Bramin." His voice took on an even harder edge. "Frankly," he said, "that's what I'd imagine *you*, of all people, would want to know."

Koos gave him a look that would have withered cactus, turned on his heel, and went inside the shack. I heard the phone dial being spun.

"Calling his boss," Cooke said.

"The police?"

Cooke laughed shortly. "Hell, no," he said. "Sam Bramin. That's why Koos is on the case. He's a big wheel in the Defenders, behind the scenes. That's the reason Bramin got him here, to look out for Defender interests."

Trooper Hailey came spluttering up the ladder. He had the .45 I'd thrown into the harbor after taking it away from Wessel. "Found this, too," said Hailey.

"There's a blanket inside," I told him. He chattered his thanks and trotted into the shack.

"How's Miss Charity?" Miles asked.

"Sleeping," I said. "The doc put her out. Said she'll be fine in the morning."

"Glad to hear it," he said. "You know, she left a roll of film down at the station."

I had forgotten about the pictures she clicked off in the Bijou. "I'll pick it up for her," I said. Miles shrugged and I followed him inside the shack. Koos was still on the telephone.

"Somebody must know where he is," he said. He saw us enter, dropped his voice. "Well, I'm out at the pier. He can call me here."

"As long as we're here," said Miles Cooke, "we might as well look around a little."

"Oh, now, wait a minute," said Koos. "I can't permit that."

Cooke peered at him. "*You* can't permit it?" he said softly.

Koos backed off. "I mean, you need a warrant."

Cooke shook his head. "Not now. A private citizen discovered evidence in a murder case. On this property."

Taking a leaf from my book, Koos said, "Not on *this* property. It was in the harbor."

Cooke smiled. "The rope was attached to this property. Isn't that so, Hailey?"

The young trooper, struggling into his uniform, said, "Yes, sir."

"So," said Cooke, "we've got a right—in fact, a

99

duty—to look around. You can see how that is, can't you, Koos?"

"Sam Bramin isn't going to like it," said Koos.

"That breaks my heart," said Miles Cooke. I started liking him again. I even thought of telling him that I had already given the place a good search, but decided not to rub salt in Koos's wound.

It was just as well that I did. Because, as thorough as my search had been, I had missed something important.

Hailey let out a whoop. He was in one of the other sheds—the one with the baling machine. We dashed over and found him standing in one corner, vomiting. When I saw what he'd discovered, I felt like joining him.

"I checked in . . . baling machine," he choked. "Found another bale. Hoisted it up. Look—" He bent over again and tried to heave the rest of his guts up.

Where I had seen only four bales, now there was a fifth. It had been hauled up by a chain hoist to where it swayed, head-high, above the maw of the baling machine.

This fifth bale was two-thirds shredded books and one-third Sam Bramin.

He had been loaded into the machine, the shredded paper piled on top, then the sides of the baler squeezed in and the steel tapes tightened. Bramin had been pressed down to around half his former size. His body bulged out from the four straps that held the bale, congealed blood hanging in ropy strands. Dangling down on its heavy chain, his gold watch swayed back and forth. His face wasn't showing, thank God.

"Mother of Mercy," Miles Cooke whispered.

For a long time, the only sound in the room was the retching of the young trooper.

I've seen some bad sights, but this was the worst. Someone had really wanted to make Bramin suffer.

"I've got to make a call," said Lieutenant Koos. Cooke nodded, without looking away from the hideous bale. Koos went out. Cooke touched the trooper's shoulder gently.

"Go outside, son," he said. "Get some air."

Hailey nodded and staggered from the shed. Cooke looked up at the obscene sausage of flesh and torn clothing that had been Sam Bramin.

"Ben," he said, "this thing is way out of hand. Everything seems to be slipping away from me. Boats blown up in the harbor—firebombs in the town square—and now this." I didn't answer; he didn't expect me to. "I need help. I need smart help, with experience in this kind of violence. Help I can trust." As he said this he nodded toward the other shack where Koos had gone, and put one finger to his lips.

"I agree," I told him. "Get hold of the Attorney General. Lay it out for him. He can get Koos off your back and give you a man without a conflict of interests."

Cooke shook his head. "Can't be done," he said. "Believe me, this town is so wound up in politics and backroom deals that it'd mean my job to blow the whistle. Half of the time I have to look the other way to keep from being faced with a decision that would only put me out of a job without doing any good."

"If that's the way you're going to do your job," I said, "maybe you'd be better off without it."

"Maybe so," he said. "But Pilgrim's Pride wouldn't be. Mainly, I'm a good police chief. I'm not on the take and nobody gets away with anything serious. Not even the Defenders. You saw what happened to those punks this morning. Bramin got them sprung, but they'll still come up on Disorderly."

"If you're so brave toward the Defenders," I said, "why didn't you tell me Bruno Wessel is also an ordnance sergeant in the National Guard?"

Cooke spread his hands. "I didn't want to make waves," he said. "I checked him out, he came up clean, so I didn't see any point in turning you loose on him."

"How did he come up clean? Bull Martin says he's short a couple of satchel charges."

"I know. But Wessel was nowhere near this pier yesterday morning. And the explosion wasn't caused by a satchel charge anyway. Besides, when the explosion occurred, both Wessel and Sam Bramin were sitting in the police station, getting a public assembly permit for that rally this afternoon."

"It's your party," I said. "I'm sorry, but I don't agree with you about Wessel and some other things."

"I know you don't," he said. "And maybe you're right. Anyway, that's what I meant when I said I need help. Maybe I'm not the smartest guy in the world. But I'm smart enough to yell for help when I need it. How about it?"

"I thought you didn't want outsiders meddling."

"If I swear you in as a deputy, you won't be an outsider. That way, even Koos will have to be satisfied with your status."

"Okay by me," I said. "But don't get mad if I go after Wessel. I'm not satisfied he's in the clear."

"Fair enough," said Cooke. "Hold up your hand." I did, and he was just finishing with the formal words when Koos came back into the shed.

"What the hell's going on?" Koos said.

"I've just made Shock's status official," said Cooke. "As of now he is a deputy officer of the Pilgrim's Pride police."

Koos swore. "If that isn't the typical hick way of

doing things," he said. "All the facilities of the State Police at your disposal, and you play games with deputies."

"I know," Cooke said seriously. "I'm being careful." Then he asked Koos, "Did you call my desk sergeant?"

"Me?" said Koos. "Hell, no. Why would I be calling your desk sergeant?"

"To report the murder," said Cooke. "That's what *I* would have been doing. Who did you call?"

"That's my business."

"Just the answer I expected," said Miles Cooke. "All right, Koos. Now we both know the score. Shock here is working for me. Officially. This is our responsibility. Your authority is limited to cooperating with local authority. That means me—period. Do you get my meaning?"

Koos just glared, turned, and stomped out.

"Watch out for him, Ben," Cooke warned. "He came down here with the understanding that he'd be running the show. Now, with Bramin dead, he may be angling for the top job in the Defenders himself. He's pretty high up there."

"I'll watch him," I said. "Meanwhile, I have this overpowering urge to speak with Bruno Wessel. Where does he live?"

"High Street," he said. "Turn left at the square. You can't miss it. His house is the big white one, third in from the corner."

We went back to the shed where my gear was. Koos was on the phone again when we came in. He hung up and sneered.

"Your department down in New York is none too happy about your moonlighting," he told me. "In fact, their orders are for you to pack up and get your ass back to the city."

"I'll believe that from my captain," I said.

He indicated the phone. "Call him."

"Why didn't you keep him on the line?"

"I wasn't talking to him. I spoke with a friend in the Commissioner's office. He'll pass the word to your captain."

"You don't know my captain," I said. I debated whether to let Koos have one right in the middle of his sneer. Instead, I gathered my equipment and took it out to the Fleetwood. The young trooper was standing near the car, holding a cigarette with a shaking hand.

"Don't let it throw you," I said. "The man who says he's never barfed at a sight like that is a liar."

"Sure," he said. "But right now I'm wondering if I went into the wrong line of work."

I clapped his shoulder and piled the equipment into the trunk. He'd be all right. But he'd have to work it out for himself.

"Tell Cooke I'll call in, will you?" I asked, saving myself a trip back to that awful scene in the shed.

"Glad to," he said. "Are you going to be working with us officially?"

"As of now," I said, "I am the latest unpaid deputy officer of Pilgrim's Pride. Lieutenant Koos was delighted."

"Screw Koos," Hailey said. "I don't have anything against a man's politics, but I don't think Koos should be allowed to mix something like the American Defenders with a career of law enforcement."

"Neither do I," I agreed, "but when we tell him he can't join the Defenders, the next thing you know we can tell him that he can't join the Republican Party. That's the trouble with democracy: everyone's free to do exactly what he wants."

"I guess so," Hailey said. He waved as I backed the Fleetwood out.

I looked at my watch; nine-twenty-nine. My stomach

rumbled. It was long past chow time. As soon as I finished with Wessel I would find out where the local sirloin action was and tie into a sixteen-ouncer along with the largest Maine potato in existence, drenched with sour cream and chives.

Even on a policeman's salary, I manage to do well in the groceries department. That is one of the great attractions between Charity and me: we both enjoy our food. I hated to think of eating without her, but if Dr. Jordan's predictions were of any value, she'd be out of action for at least the rest of the night. And there was no point in wearing sackcloth and eating ashes just because she couldn't make the scene.

Daydreaming of sirloins, I overshot the Wessel house. I pulled over and parked the Fleetwood. I took the keys out, but left the windows open to what small breeze there was.

A small sportscar—a Triumph—had just pulled up in front of Wessel's house. I slowed my approach. It might be interesting to know who was visiting him before I barged in.

A slim figure dashed up the steps and rang the doorbell. I paused behind a convenient tree and waited for the bell to be answered.

When it was, a shaft of light from inside fell across the face of Leslie Tucker.

I wondered what Lyon's stepson was doing consorting with the likes of Bruno Wessel. So instead of doing the honorable thing and asking for admittance like a gentleman, I sneaked around to the side of the house and spied through the window.

The two men were obviously having an argument of some kind. Leslie was ranting and waving his arms, and Wessel kept trying to shush him into a chair. Finally, Leslie turned and headed for the door. Wessel went after him, and they passed out of view.

I slipped around the corner of the house to watch Leslie when he came out. But he didn't emerge. I waited for a couple of minutes, then went back to my window view. Now the room was dark. Backing off far enough to see the second story, I saw a light shining from a window.

My curiosity was raging. I haven't climbed a tree since grade school, but I made it up the rough trunk of an oak near the house in a couple of minutes, with the rasping bark chewing at my summer suit. There was a large branch near enough to the window to give me a vantage point, and I crawled out on it.

The shades weren't drawn, and I saw that the room within was a bedroom; a huge double bed was directly under the window.

As I watched, it sagged. Then the bearlike figure of Bruno Wessel rolled into view.

He was buck naked. I didn't particularly want to see what came next, but it happened before I could retreat from my perch.

Leslie Tucker—just as nude as Wessel, and sexually aroused—crawled over to the bear-man and embraced him. Wessel's hand reached up and clutched the boy's back, and that was all I stayed to see. I slid down the tree so fast that a snag caught one pocket and ruined my beautiful new jacket.

I didn't care. I had decided to postpone my interview with Wessel.

When I got back to the Tucker house, Paul let me in. I went directly to my room, where I showered and kept scrubbing long after all traces of the salt water were gone. It was as if I had been immersed in a filthier muck than the harbor mud, and somehow it wouldn't come off.

TWELVE

Showered and dressed in my second-best suit, I went up to see Charity. Her stepmother was no longer in the room. Charity stirred as I entered. I hadn't intended to turn on a light, but when she gasped, I did.

I flicked on a dim bed lamp. "It's me, baby. Ben."

She spoke in a small, strange voice: "Why am I in bed? What happened?"

"You had a little trouble. Nothing to worry about. Good old Doc Jordan gave you a sedative. That's why you're in bed."

She spoke again in that same strange, small voice. "What was George Groat doing here?"

"Who, baby?"

"But he couldn't have been, could he? George is in California."

Now I realized that Charity was in the trance-like state Doc Jordan had warned me to expect. Her mind was back somewhere, sleepwalking among old memories. I knew I should turn out the light and leave. But that old alarm bell in my head was going off again.

"Charity?" I said. No answer. I reached deeper. "Elizabeth?"

"Yes?"

"Elizabeth, who is George Groat?"

"Just a boy."

"A boy in California?"

"That's right. A friend."

Her eyes were open, but she was asleep.

"Your friend?"

"No. He's Leslie's friend. But he's not allowed to come to the house anymore."

"How old is he, Elizabeth?"

"Sixteen. I think."

"How old are you?"

"Going on twelve."

"Have you seen George since you left California?"

That didn't work. She had peeled the mental onion down to the layer that corresponded to her girlhood. At that point in time, she hadn't left California.

"Tell me more about George, Elizabeth," I said, wishing that I didn't have to do this.

"Oh, he's just a boy."

"There must be something special about him. Is he tall?"

"Sort of tall. Taller than Leslie."

"What color are his eyes?"

"Gray, I think."

"What color is his hair?"

"Black."

"Is he a good boy or a bad boy?"

She didn't answer. I asked the question again. Finally she said, "He's wild, but he's nice."

"What does your mother say about him?"

She frowned. "Mama's sick," she said. "That's why I stay with Aunt Bethesda. Mama needs lots of quiet and so I play with Leslie and Scarlett."

"Does George play with them too?"

A shake of her head. "No. But he's Leslie's secret friend. Like I said." She sighed, and her head dropped off to one side. She was really asleep now. I crept out of the room feeling like a louse.

Downstairs, I met Paul in the hallway. "Miss Charity hungry?" he asked.

"She's asleep."

He seemed puzzled. "But when the man from the

police came a while ago she was as wide awake and chipper as could be."

"What man?"

"The man who brought the photographs. Miss Charity woke up earlier and telephoned him, and he came right over with the pictures."

"Where are they?"

"I took them up to her. They should be on the desk in her room."

I thanked him and padded up the stairs again. I crept back into her room and risked turning on the light once more. This time she didn't stir. I searched the room carefully. There weren't any photographs except the usual family ones.

Then, on a hunch, I went down the hall to the next bedroom. I tapped gently at the door. There wasn't any answer. I tapped again, then let myself in.

This was obviously Leslie's room. The clothing in the closet was too young to belong to Lyon Tucker. I rummaged around without any success. Then, in the bathroom, I got lucky.

It was down inside the toilet tank, a favorite hiding place for amateurs. A tiny film can and, inside it, a small strip of 16-mm negative. I held the strip up to the light. The images were too small for me to make anything out of them. But I could tell that they were probably of the stage in the Bijou Theater.

A more careful search did not produce the prints. They had probably been torn up and flushed. I put the strip of negative in my breast pocket and replaced the film can in the tank. Then I slipped out of the room and headed down to the parking lot.

It was now well after ten, and my dreams of a medium-rare sirloin were fast dwindling. I eased the Fleetwood down the hill to Bruno Wessel's house on High Street, where I applied my thumb to the doorbell and leaned on it for five minutes. No one, not even Wessel, could have been that asleep. And the sleek little Triumph was gone from out front. My lovebirds had flown.

There was one other visit I still had to make. Once again I drove over the railroad tracks into Shame Town. The streets, bordered by darkened houses, seemed so tense that you might have plucked them and sounded a high C. The few people who were on the sidewalks stared at me with obvious hostility. It reminded me of the way I had felt slipping down a narrow road between hills harboring Viet Cong.

I arrived at the Bijou Theater without incident and parked the Fleetwood in front of the boarded-up box office. I didn't bother locking up. It wouldn't have taken much more to finish bashing in the right-hand window, anyway.

The glare of a streetlight cast my shadow in front of me. The shadow walked into the lobby, through the half-opened doors, and I followed.

As I stepped inside, strong hands grabbed me. A voice warned, "Cool it, man, or you'll get hurt."

I didn't struggle—I wasn't here to fight. The hands rummaged through my pockets. They found the .38 and the Philippine fighting knife. Then one of the men flipped open my wallet and flashed the tin badge.

"He's fuzz, all right," said a voice.

They hustled me down the aisle, toward the stage. The single, dangling lightbulb had been restored. The chair was still there, and in it sat the man I had seen here before, and then downtown, seizing the microphone from Bruno Wessel. He was still dressed in the all-leather outfit.

"Let the man go," he said. My captors released my arms.

"My name's Shock," I began.

110

"We know," he said. "Benjamin Lincoln Shock of the NYPD. We've had you checked out, Sergeant."

"And I've had *you* checked out, George," I said.

He inclined his head slightly. "Around here they call me Guru Goat."

"That may be what they call you, but you're really George Groat."

The legs of his chair thumped to the floor. "Where did you hear that?"

"We fuzz have our ways."

He laughed and snapped his fingers. "Right on, man. Hey, out there, let's have a couple of brews for me and the man." Feet scurried. Pop tops popped. Two icy-cold cans of beer were passed up to us. I lifted mine.

"Here's to Peace," I said.

"Crazy."

We sipped. The beer was as good as it was cold.

"The reports we got on you," he said, "say you're not the typical pig cop."

"But I *am* a cop," I reminded him. "I know you've got a lot of grief on your side, but laws are made for you, too."

"A lot of them are made *specially* for us," he said. "We're trying to do our own thing, live and let live. But the uptight good citizens say 'No dice.' We've got to live their way or not at all. Then they demonstrate how great their way is by squeezing us every rotten way they can." He swigged at his beer. "Our shacks look halfway livable from the outside. You can't see the rats and the roaches and the vermin. Did you know that just last month a little baby asleep in his crib had half his ear chewed away by a rat?" He spat a mouthful of beer onto the stage. "Don't talk to me about laws."

"Don't put down a system that gives you the freedom to attack it."

"I'm not putting it down," he said. "What I'm trying to do is convince you that this is *my* country, too."

"Is that why you dress up like a Martian?"

He grinned. "Flashy trapping for the tribe, man. I don't really believe in all this junk, but it gives the troops a flag to rally around."

"So in rebelling against conformity you create your own uniforms and marching order. Where do you think it'll end?"

He shrugged. "We've got to do our thing, Sergeant. If you won't cooperate, then we're going to have to push you to the wall."

"Just like you pushed Lyon Tucker?"

"I told you before, we didn't have anything to do with those old people getting blown up."

"Somebody did. Let's lay it out, Guru. I hear that your outfit has a seventy-five-millimeter recoilless rifle."

"Where did you hear that?"

"Say a friend."

"That wouldn't be the same friend we caught snooping around once too often, just before he decided to move back to Chicago, would it?"

So that was what happened to Cooke's informant. "Could be," I said. "But anyway you slice it, that's pretty heavy hardware. What does Body and Soul need with a seventy-five?"

"I told you, man, we don't have any such animal. If you're looking for heavy ordnance like that, you better have a talk with Sam Bramin. His man Wessel is the chief bottlewasher for the National Guard. If anybody in town could get his hands on a seventy-five, Bramin is it."

"Maybe he was," I said. "But not any more."

"What do you mean by that?"

"Somebody crammed Bramin into his own baling machine and turned it on."

Guru put down his beer slowly. "He's dead?"

"Completely," I said, remembering the mashed body with the steel bands cutting into it.

"Any idea who did it?"

"Not a clue."

"Hell," he said. "That means they'll try to pin it on us."

"Unless you help me point it some other way."

He snapped his fingers. "Let's have two more brews." Someone scurried into the darkness. "Sergeant," he said, "there's something I don't dig about this whole scene. The hip folks didn't have it too bad here until just a little while ago. Not until your Mr. Tucker hooked up with Sam Bramin."

"I understand you knew Tucker in California," I said casually.

He laughed harshly. "Not on your life. The Tuckers and the Groats, they didn't mix socially. Oh, he had a big mouth about everybody's rights, but that's as far as it went."

"Why would Leslie Tucker want to steal a photograph of you?"

He grinned. "Now that's a horse of a different color. I knew Leslie when we were kids. He was always a scared little shrimp, but he's all right."

"The photograph?"

"Search me, man. Maybe he's got the hots for me. I hear he swings for boys these days."

The beer arrived. I swigged at mine. Now it seemed flat and tasteless. It was time to go. I'd confirmed my suspicions: Guru Goat of Shame Town was also George Groat of California. So what?

I asked for my hardware back. Guru waved a hand

113

and my .38 reappeared. "How about the knife?" I said.

Guru snapped his fingers. "Okay, who's got the blade?"

One of the men stepped forward and held out the knife. "I didn't think he'd miss it," he mumbled.

Guru rolled his eyes. "Oh, man," he said, "what *am* I going to do with you cats?"

He raised his beer to me in a mock toast. Then, with a *whoomphing* sound, he rose into the air, beer can still raised. He was seated in space, seeming to float across the stage toward me. It was like some outrageous dream. I knew that things were happening much faster than they seemed to be, that the world had gone into the slow motion it always assumes in moments of crisis. Everything moved in graceful arcs, spreading out from one wall where a strange orange blossom of flame had appeared.

Then the dream became a nightmare. The orange blossom was the violent burst of an explosion that nearly tore the theater apart. I threw myself down on the stage and felt debris cascading over my body. There goes my other good suit, I thought, ignoring the strong possibility that maybe there went Ben Shock as well.

A blast of heat swept over me. I staggered to my feet and found Guru Goat rolled up in a fetal position near the back wall. I grabbed him under the armpits and pulled him toward the side exit. It was jammed. I dropped Guru and booted it open with my right foot, then caught his collar and dragged him outside like a sack of potatoes. I dumped him on the sidewalk and ran back inside.

The flames were licking along the curtains, slowed by the fire-resistant fabric. I found one of the Body and Soul men staggering around, blood pouring down

114

his face. I took his arm and steered him toward the exit. Halfway through it, I collided with Guru. He pulled the bleeding man outside.

"Take it easy, George," I said. "You may be hurt."

His voice grated. "Don't mess with me, pig."

I didn't mess with him. I went back inside. The smoke and flames were worse now. I wheezed my way through them and stumbled over a body. When I grabbed an arm to pull the man up, it came off in my hand. I dropped it and started choking on my own puke. My smug words to Trooper Hailey came back to me. I blundered into a wall and reeled backward toward the flames. Hands caught my arm and guided me outside. On the sidewalk I saw that I had been rescued by Guru Goat. Fair enough.

Sirens wailed and a big red fire engine rumbled up. It was manned by four volunteers, dressed in a mixture of sports clothing and pajamas.

A crowd of hippies had gathered around the burning building. They shouted among themselves; but now that the firemen were here, there was a focus to their anger. They started moving in on the fire engine. One boy picked up a rock and bounced it off the shiny red truck.

"Stop them!" I shouted at Guru. "Those men are here to help. Don't let things get any worse."

I could see the confusion on his face. There was blind anger, as he looked at the burning building. Then, through the anger, the cool leader emerged again. He shook his head, as if to clear the dizziness from his mind, and then leaped up to the running board of the fire truck.

"Knock it off!" he shouted. "These firemen aren't our enemies. Let them do their jobs!"

All the shouting and chaos had filled the night with dancing shadows and violent sound. And soon, when it was all over, the old theater was gutted. Two body and Soul were dead—the man I'd stumbled over on the stage, and one who had been working in the cellar.

By now Miles Cooke had arrived, accompanied by Henry Koos. During Guru Goat's informal roll call to see who was missing, Koos made an obvious point out of writing down the names. Once, Guru blocked his path. There was a moment of tension; then Koos stepped around him.

"What happened, Ben?" Cooke asked.

I told him. His lips tightened. He cursed under his breath.

Bull Martin drove up.

"The Town Council called me," he told Cooke. "They thought they might be forced to request the Guard to put down the disturbance."

"Damn their itchy britches," said Cooke, "there's no disturbance to put down."

"I heard there was an explosion," Martin said.

"Did you hear what caused it?" said Cooke. Martin shook his head. "No," Cooke growled, "and neither did anyone else, because up to now, nobody *knows* what caused it. Could have been a gas leak, could have been anything. So let's not go calling out the Guard and making things worse. Let's try to stay calm."

"Serves the bastards right," Koos said, looking at a terribly still form wrapped in a smoldering blanket. "These punks have been asking for this for a long time."

"Koos," said Cooke, " you have a very big mouth."

His comment didn't faze the state cop. Koos just smiled at the Chief and turned away.

"I'd better get back to town and see what the hell the Council's up to," Cooke told me. "Those idiots might be on the phone right now, asking the Governor to call out the troops." He got back in his car. Unasked, Koos piled in too. Cooke scratched gravel taking off. I went over to the tight little group of Body and Soul men.

Guru Goat was talking. "Those goddam Defenders did this," he said. "No doubt in my mind. And man, this is the blowoff."

One of the men spoke. "This whole bummer town has asked for it."

Guru nodded slowly. "That's the scene. This lousy town has had it."

Then he looked at me and said, "Buzz off, pig. We don't want you around here."

I buzzed off.

THIRTEEN

My appetite had vanished, so it took no great willpower to drive past the Pilgrim's Pride Diner. I stopped in briefly at the police station to see if the photo technician was on duty. He wasn't. I would have to wait until morning to see what was so interesting on that tiny strip of negative from Charity's camera.

I considered dropping in on Bruno Wessel again. But it was late and I was bone-tired. Even Supercop has to rest sometime. I turned the Fleetwood up the hill to the Tucker house and parked.

Leslie's nifty little Triumph was there. Lyon Tucker's Continental was not. I checked my watch. Well after midnight. I wished I had a key. I hated to ring the doorbell at this hour.

I didn't have to. The door opened noiselessly and Paul came out.

"I saw you coming up the hill, Mr. Shock," he said.

"Sorry to bother you," I said.

"No bother at all," he said. "Everybody knows how hard you're trying to straighten out this mess. I bet you were over at that fire in Shame Town."

"Right."

He indicated my suit. "That could stand with a bit of a brushup. You put it outside your door tonight and I'll have it ready for you first thing in the morning. I'm better than any dry cleaner in town."

"Thanks," I said.

"I laid out some sandwiches in case you might be hungry. And there's some cold beer."

Suddenly my appetite was back.

"That's great," I said. "But I don't want to keep you up."

"I've got to wait up for Mr. Tucker anyway."

"He's not in?" I said, knowing the answer.

"No sir. He went out around nine. He said he could be reached at the TV station."

The sandwiches were waiting, nestled down in a bed of white napkins. Paul popped the top of a beer, and I washed the soot out of my throat with it.

There is a mystique between ham and cheese when joined between slabs of the right kind of rye bread that brings majesty to their breed. And Paul's ham-and-cheese sandwiches fulfilled that destiny.

As I ate, Paul said, "I sure hope you don't think all the folks in town are like those Defenders and the Body and Soul."

"I don't." I bit into another sandwich. He pushed a second beer in front of me.

"There's going to be trouble," he said. "If folks don't learn to let each other be, there's bad trouble coming up."

"That's the way I see it, too," I agreed.

"All this violence and killing," he went on. "That ain't going to accomplish anything. All it did was kill those old folks. The Garrets never hurt nobody. They just lived their quiet lives in their little retirement place up in Rockport and then some no-gooder goes and kills them for no reason at all except—" He stopped suddenly. "Excuse me, Mr. Shock. I got to go. I think I hear Mr. Tucker's car coming up the hill." He hurried out and left me there, my sandwich still held high in one hand.

I wondered what he had started to tell me about the Garrets.

119

FOURTEEN

I knew I was dreaming, but that didn't make the nightmare any more pleasant. I was running the gauntlet between two long lines of shouting men. One line was Body and Soul and the other, American Defenders. They all held knives and as I ran past they slashed at me. One blade carried away my jacket pocket. Another sliced my necktie in half.

Just as it looked as if I would escape, Guru Goat came flying through the air at me, beer can raised high in a mock toast. As he hit me there was the sound of a shot, and I woke up in a cold sweat. I looked around the room stupidly and then there came another shot, this one right outside my window. I slipped out of bed and poked my head cautiously past the edge of the curtain. Looking down the street, I felt silly as hell.

A pack of kids were going by, tossing little firecrackers up in the air, where they exploded with a pistol-like sound. The kids were getting a jump on the holiday—the Fourth wasn't until tomorrow.

Not that there wouldn't be plenty of action today. I didn't look forward to the morning's activities. After a brief ceremony at the Rockport Baptist Church, the Garrets would be buried in Seacliff Cemetery, overlooking the blue Atlantic.

In my years on the Force, I've seen my share of violent death. But this was the first time I had to go to the funeral. It was a first I could have done without.

There was a tap at the door. I slipped into my robe and said, "Come in."

Paul entered, my suit over his arm. "You forgot to put this out for me last night," he said. "So I took it this morning without disturbing you. I'm afraid there are some small burns I couldn't do anything with. But it'll get you through the day."

I thanked him and he said, "Miss Charity is very anxious to speak with you, sir."

"Is she up?"

"She's waiting for you in her room."

I thanked him again and he went out. I made short work of shaving with my souped-up Schick electric—I'd had an electrician buddy rewire the motor to give it twice the usual pep—then took a quick shower and dressed. Paul had done a good job—the suit looked like it came fresh from the cleaner's.

When I tapped at Charity's door, I heard her say, "Damn it!"

I pushed the door open. "Is that supposed to mean 'Come in'?"

She rushed over and hugged me. "Oh, Ben. It's so good to see you."

"How do you feel?"

"Frisky as a colt. I don't know what Doc Jordan puts in his needles, but I could learn to like it."

"Do you remember much about what happened?"

She shook her head. "Only feeling disassociated as we rode back from the pier. Now I know what they meant in the old novels when they said someone was 'beside himself.' Because that's exactly how I felt—as if I had come out of my body and was sitting there, literally beside myself, observing everything that went on but not being involved in it all." She kissed my lips gently. "Thank you, Ben. I couldn't have gone through that hospital routine again."

"What were you cursing about when I came in?"

"Oh, damn!" she said again. "I'm positive I had

121

some photographs here. The ones I took of that man in the theater. The police technician brought them over last night. I wanted to look at them again and show them to you."

"Do you remember looking at them last night?" I asked.

"No, not really," she said. "I know I *did,* but I can't really remember what I saw. I was pretty groggy."

I took out the strip of negative. She held it up to the light. "This is the film I use," she said. "It's sixteen-millimeter, and there are the right edge markings: Kodak four-X. The exposures look good, considering the light. Where did you get these, Ben?"

I took a deep breath. "Honey, I don't know why, but your stepbrother swiped the pictures out of here. He probably destroyed the prints. I found the negative stashed in the tank of the john."

"Why would Leslie do that?"

I didn't know. She argued a little, then shrugged and seemed to accept what I had told her. Holding the film up to the light, she said, "I hate these little negatives. I can't read them."

There were four separate pictures on the tiny strip of film. All four looked alike to me, and I said as much.

"No," she said. "The man in the chair is in all of them, but frame two's got another man in the background."

"Can you tell who it is?"

"Not a chance. I'm doing well to even tell there's a second person there at all. We'll just have to get some more blowups made."

"Well, I already know who the first man is," I said. "He's an old buddy of yours from California, George Groat, better known around here as Guru Goat."

"Ben! How'd you find that out?"

"You told me. Last night. You must have recognized him in the photos. So I went over to the Bijou and he confirmed it."

"George Groat," she said. "I haven't heard that name in years. I remember him as a tall, quiet boy who hung around with Leslie in school. Guru Goat? That's amazing."

She tucked the negative into her purse. "There's no time before the funeral," she said, "but on the way back I'll get into the police lab for a couple of minutes and blow up that second frame." She touched my arm. "Ben I'll drive back from the cemetery with you. But on the way up I'd better be with Bethesda."

"Fair enough," I said. I kissed her once and then we went down to breakfast. Leslie was there. He gave me a surly look, dabbed his mouth with his napkin, got up, and hurried from the room. I wanted to call after him that he would find his marbles in the bottom of the umbrella stand, but this didn't seem to be the moment.

Charity proved she was feeling fine by helping herself to a mound of scrambled eggs and two rashers of bacon. I gloated over her restored appetite. She finished and left to find Bethesda while I was having my third cup of coffee. I hadn't seen any sign of a cook. I wondered if Paul did those honors too. When he returned with a fresh pot of coffee, I asked him.

He laughed and shook his head. "No sir," he said. "Effie does the cooking. She's back in the kitchen."

"Well, tell her she makes the best cup of coffee on the east coast. Maybe even on the west coast."

His answering chuckle was a little strained, I thought. Or was the Shock imagination working overtime again? I watched him as he moved across the dining room and through the doors into the kitchen.

123

I sipped at my coffee, vaguely dissatisfied with something—though I wasn't sure what.

Paul reappeared. "Is there anything else I can get for you, sir?"

There wasn't. Unless you could order a cup of answers the way you do coffee. I went outside.

The cars were gathering. Leslie was driving the white Continental. Scarlett was in front with him. I waited until Lyon appeared around the side of the house, wheeling Bethesda. I opened the car door for them; then Charity came out of the house, wearing a light summer dress subdued by the black veil that hung over her face.

Leslie piled out of the front seat and pushed between me and his mother, holding out his hand to help her. Half-supported by him, she beckoned me closer. When she grasped my hand, I winced; her fingers were so strong they left white marks on my flesh. She slid onto the seat. Leslie folded up the wheelchair and put it inside. Getting in beside her stepmother, Charity turned to me. "Ben, you don't have to come to the church. Have some more coffee and meet us at the cemetery gate at eleven o'clock."

That was fine with me. And it was a polite way to avoid intruding on the privacy of the family's grief.

The cars pulled away. I lit a Kool and slid behind the wheel of the Fleetwood. As I started the engine, I looked up and caught a glimpse of Paul watching me from a third-story window, just below the widow's walk. When he saw me looking, he stepped back.

I pressed the accelerator and slid down the hill toward Route 127-A. It was only nine-thirty, and already the heat waves were shimmering off the highway. This was going to be one scorching third of July.

In the distance a firecracker went off. I felt the

124

flesh crawl on the back of my neck and I shivered, and suddenly it wasn't hot at all, it was cool . . . as cool as the earth-covered bottom of a grave.

FIFTEEN

If you happen to like cemeteries, you would probably enjoy Seacliff. Sprawled out on the slope of a high hill overlooking the ocean, it was peaceful and dignified. I am not a big cemetery man myself. Once you're gone, it doesn't make too much difference where the bones are laid. But since the real purpose of a funeral is to console the survivors, I suppose a place like Seacliff helps.

Far down the hill from the main gate, I could see the grave site. Two mounds of raw earth flanked it. The graves themselves were shielded from the summer sun by a canvas canopy. There were already fifteen or twenty people around, although the funeral procession wasn't due yet. I recognized the lanky shape of Miles Cooke, standing apart from the rest of the group.

From where I stood, I could see down the road into the town as well. Somewhere down there, in a white-steepled church, a preacher was reading words over Nora and Bart Garret. Then, with ponderous ceremony, the two coffins would be loaded into hearses and driven up the hill. When the hearses went down the hill again, they would be empty.

One big gripe I have always had with detective fiction is the casual way the landscape gets littered with dead bodies which, for all you can tell from the author's descriptions, are left there and forgotten. It is somehow overlooked that, in real life, each of those dead bodies had a family—perhaps a wife and children, a brother or sister, an uncle—who grieve, and who insist on providing decent burial.

And there's nothing easy about a funeral. It looks like what it is meant to be: a permanent solution of all the departed's woes and cares. As for me, I'd rather be alive and miserable.

Now I could see the long line of cars moving slowly up the hill. I took a final pull on my Kool and ground the butt into the gravel driveway.

Cooke gave me a nod. I went over and stood next to him.

"Any luck with Wessel?" he asked.

"I haven't been able to locate him. Did you find out what caused the explosion at the theater?"

"No," he said, "except it wasn't heating gas."

"I didn't think it was," I said. "What about the stakeout at the pier? Any takers?"

"Negative. So far we're not doing so good." His eyes flicked over my shoulder. "Oh-oh."

I looked around. Coming down the road in a military file, almost marching, were around twenty men wearing American Defender armbands.

"Tucker's going to blow his top," I said. "Can't you get them out of here?"

"It's a public place," Cooke said. "But I'll damned well keep them away from the graves." He went over and talked to the leader of the group. There was obviously some argument between them, which ended with the Defenders removing their armbands and putting them in their pockets.

Most of the funeral procession parked at the gate. Only the two hearses drove down to the grave site. The pallbearers lifted the heavy caskets and placed them on supports over the freshly dug holes. Then the mourners came down the hill in a long, straggly single file. Lyon Tucker led the procession, his craggy face pointed straight ahead. Behind him, her wheelchair pushed by Leslie, came Bethesda, followed by

Charity and Scarlett. Then a lot of people I did not know.

They clustered around the graves. The minister spoke a few words. I remained at a distance. Charity did not seem to notice me.

When the brief service was over, Leslie rolled his mother's wheelchair closer to the grave and she sprinkled a handful of earth into them. There was a long pause and everybody bowed his head.

Then I heard a mumble from the group of Defenders. I looked around. Dressed in a well-fitting black suit, Guru Goat stood a few feet away from us, looking down at the caskets.

"Get the bastard," said one of the Defenders.

They started toward Guru. Cooke moved fast. He got between Guru and the Defenders, faced the group of men.

"Just hold it right there," he said. "There's not going to be any of that stuff today."

Meanwhile, I got over to Guru. "This isn't smart," I told him. "It won't help anything."

"I know," he said, his voice oddly subdued. "But I had to come, Sergeant."

I heard cursing behind me. The Defenders had decided that if Guru remained, they would leave. That was just fine with Miles Cooke, and he watched them march sullenly up the hill.

The rest of the funeral procession was breaking up. The family remained near the grave. I watched Guru bend over and shake Bethesda's hand with a courtly, graceful gesture. Then he spoke quietly with Lyon Tucker. Charity stood apart from the little group, obviously just as puzzled as I was. She saw me standing near Cooke, gave her stepmother a gentle kiss on the cheek, then came to join me.

"Hello, Miles," she said to Cooke.

128

"Glad to see you're feeling better," he said.

She turned to me. "That's George Groat, all right," she said. "In the poor light of that theater I didn't recognize him."

"Groat?" said Cooke. "How do you know?"

Charity told him Groat had been a school friend of Leslie's, back in California.

"That's interesting," said the Chief. "What's on his mind?"

"Nothing particular," said Charity. "He told my stepmother how nice the Garrets were to him in California and how sorry he is about her loss."

"You may not win any medals for it, Chief," I said, "but I think you ought to see that he gets home safely. Look up there."

Cooke looked up the hill. The Defenders had put on their armbands again and were waiting just outside the cemetery gate.

Cooke sighed. "Ben," he said "I told you yesterday about how I sometimes wake up in the night and hear the fuse sizzling? Well, now I can hear it in the daytime. This town's about ready to go up." He nodded toward Guru. "Except for him, there's not a Body and Soul to be found anywhere in Pilgrim's Pride. Something bad is coming."

"Maybe you ought to let the Town Council have its way and call in the Guard."

He almost shook his head off. "Not while I'm in charge. They can always go against my recommendation. But the minute they do, I resign. I told them that last night. Ben, you know the Guard wouldn't head off trouble—it would *generate* it. You get those untrained kids out there in the streets with their bullets and tear gas, and they'd draw disaster like a magnet."

He broke off the conversation. "Excuse me," he said to Charity. "I'd better get moving."

Guru Goat was heading up the hill. Cooke joined him. As I'd expected, Guru protested, but Cooke would have none of it. He walked beside the young man, up the hill through the ranks of the fuming American Defenders. They crowded in on the two men, but made no threatening gestures. Guru and Cooke both got into the Mercury and drove away.

"Ben," Charity said, "let's get out of here. This place spooks me. And I want to get down to the station and make a blowup of that negative."

"What about your folks?"

"I'll say good-bye and meet you at your car."

I went up and started the Fleetwood. On my way, a couple of Defenders muttered under their breath at me. Nice boys. I fought down a powerful urge to kick them where it would hurt most.

When Charity passed, they were very charming, all sympathy. She smiled, stopped, and touched one of the armbands. "When one of my handkerchiefs gets *this* dirty," she said sweetly, "I always send it to the laundry."

She switched her behind at them and slipped into the car. The Defenders stood there with their mouths open.

"Okay, chum," she said as we drove back toward town, "now that I have returned from the Twilight Zone, fill me in."

I told her about the fracas in the town square; about discovering the 75-mm and Sam Bramin's body. About the explosion at Body and Soul headquarters. I told her everything except the tryst I'd witnessed between Leslie and Bruno Wessel. She listened thoughtfully, her lips pursed.

"You did all right, Shock," she said. "But you made a few boo-boos."

"Hold on there, baby," I said. "Do I tell you how to run your cameras?"

"Whenever you get the chance," she said good-naturedly. "Maybe your biggest mistake was getting involved with a pushy dame like me. But it's too late to change that now. What you *can* do is catch up with a few other of the little boo-boos before they turn into real disasters."

I mashed the gas pedal down and burned up a couple of miles. "Okay, smart-ass. *What* boo-boos?"

"One," she said, holding up her finger. "You found a seventy-five-millimeter recoilless rifle in the harbor. And decided to leave it there as bait."

"What's wrong with that?"

"Nothing," she said. "But whose seventy-five is it? Body and Soul's? Or maybe someone else's?"

"If I knew that I wouldn't have to play the bait game."

"Why didn't you have the serial numbers checked?"

I gripped the wheel and thought ungentlemanly things about Monday morning quarterbacks. But she was right. It had been a serious oversight not to take down the numbers.

"Score one for the pushy dame," I said. "What else?"

She ticked off another finger. "You've been acting on the assumption that whoever sank *Channel Nine* was really after my father and that the murder of the Garrets is linked to him."

"What makes you think otherwise?" I asked.

"Maybe someone was actually after *them*, not my father."

"That," I said, "would change the name of the game."

"Ben, it's worth considering."

"But why the hell would anyone want to knock off

131

two nice old grandparents?" I said. "Be reasonable, baby."

"You may be the boy whiz in detective matters," she said, "but maybe you're locking onto a theory first and then bending the facts to fit it."

I grumbled some more and then we were in Pilgrim's Pride. I let her off at the police station without getting out of the car myself.

She gave me a knowing smile. "Are you going somewhere, Ben?"

"Yeah, I'm going somewhere," I said. "I'm going to the goddamned muddy bottom of this goddamned freezing harbor and look at some goddamned numbers, that's where's I'm going."

"Be careful," she said. I waved and drove away.

There was a cop on stakeout, hiding in Sam Bramin's office. It took a little arguing to persuade him that I was authorized to haul up the 75. There wasn't any light grapple to be found—I didn't think there would be—and I had to strip down and lower myself into the frigid water. Instead of diving for the weapon, I went down the leg of the piling and got hold of the line. I surfaced with it, climbed back up the slippery ladder, and hauled up the 75. After I had copied down the serial number, under the trigger housing, I heaved the weapon back into the harbor. It made a loud splash and sank out of sight.

I went inside and asked Information for Colonel Martin's telephone number. The operator gave it to me after advising that it was listed in my directory, and I dialed. It rang eight times without answer. I hung up, lifted the receiver, and dialed again. Same result.

I dressed, put the serial number in the watch pocket of my pants, and drove downtown to the police station. The desk sergeant pointed me in the right direction and I found the improvised darkroom. I tapped on the door and was let in through two sets of hanging black curtains. The room, dimly lit by a pale yellow safelight, reeked of chemicals.

"I'm Art Booth," said the photo technician. "Miss Charity said you'd be around."

"Where is she?"

He shrugged. "We made a print from that little negative she brought in. Bitch of a job. It was only sixteen-millimeter to begin with, and with that contrast and the grain, it was a doozy, I can tell you."

"Please," I suggested, "just tell me where she went."

"No idea," he said cheerfully. "She took one look at the print and lit out of here like a rocket. She said to tell you that you weren't the only one who had been bending facts to fit theories." He thought for a moment, then added. "Whatever *that* means."

I knew that if I drowned him in his own hypo bath, no judge in the country would have convicted me. But I kept my voice level.

"Is that all? Didn't she say anything else?"

"Only that she'd see you at the house." He fussed around with his smelly chemicals. I waited. He looked up. "That's all."

"What about the print?"

"She took it with her."

I thanked him and, dripping sweat, left the stuffy little room. At the desk, I tried Bull Martin's phone again. No luck.

My route led too close to High Street for me to pass up the chance of catching Bruno Wessel at home. This time I was lucky. The air conditioner mounted in the living-room window was grinding away. I leaned on the doorbell. When he opened the door he stepped back instantly and tried to slam it in my face, but by then my size ten was in the way.

133

"Official business, Wessel," I told him.

He sneered. "You don't have any muscle up here," he said.

"I do now. Cooke put me on the force."

"You still need a warrant."

"Not if you invite me in."

"Shove it," he said.

"I can stand out here then and tell the neighborhood about your little session with Leslie Tucker," I said loudly. "I can tell the world about that little crescent scar on your left shoulder and—"

That was as far as I got. He almost pulled me inside. The hallway was hot and dark.

"I don't admit anything," he said. "But you've got a lot of gall, shooting off your mouth like that."

"Let's go into the living room," I said. "It'll be more comfortable."

It was, thanks to the big air conditioner. He had quite a room. Framed photographs of himself lined the walls and covered the tables. Wessel shaking hands with Sam Bramin; Wessel in full uniform on a podium flanked by American flags. There were also framed newspaper clippings. I went over and read one. It described a demonstration in Philadelphia at which "American Defender Bruno Wessel challenged the Administration on the civil rights act, describing it as 'creeping Communism' and demanding a national referendum."

"Amazing," I said. "Who writes your speeches, Bruno?"

"You got a big mouth, Shock," he said. "Why don't you flap it some and let me know what you want?"

"I suppose you heard what happened to the late, great Sam Bramin."

"Yeah, I heard," he said. "Koos—" He stopped, obviously remembering that he wasn't supposed to talk about Lieutenant Koos in connection with Defender activities.

"What were you going to say?"

"I heard," he mumbled lamely.

"You know," I suggested, "you could be next."

"Me?" he yelled. "How do you figure? Bramin was way out of line. He was just using the movement. I don't know who finished him off, but it was the best thing that ever happened to the Defenders. They wouldn't go after me. I'm straight."

It hurt, but I laughed. "Straight as a snake. How do you think the movement would feel about being run by a fag?"

"Shut your trap," he snapped. "I ought to flatten you—"

"Go right ahead," I said, waiting. I hoped he would try. Instead, he lowered his fist and sank down in a big leather chair.

"I never did nothing like that before," he muttered. "The kid came over and was yelling about this and that, and I played along to shut him up."

"Bruno," I said, "your lousy sex life bores me. I only care about it because it links you to the one family in town you should be interested in staying ten miles away from. Why? What's the tie-up between you and Leslie? Is he in the movement?"

"That queen?" he snarled. "We wouldn't let his sort inside the fence."

"Then what was your tie-up with him?"

"You saw it," he said. "What are you fishing around for? What else do you want from me?"

I changed my tack. "How about the satchel charges, Bruno? Did you give them to Bramin?"

"I don't know anything about those charges," he said. "Two came up missing. That's all I know. I turned in the report to the Colonel. Ask Cooke. He

135

checked me out on that and I came up clean."

"Tell me again," I said. "I like to hear for myself."

"Anybody could have taken them. There must be ten guys with keys to the arsenal."

"When were they taken?"

"Who knows? I did an inventory last Saturday and noticed they were gone."

"Is that when you reported it to Martin?" He hesitated. "Well?"

"I forgot. I meant to turn it in then, but it slipped my mind."

"When did you remember?" He didn't answer. "Did your memory improve *after* the Tucker boat was blown out of the water?"

Still no answer. "I can always get it from the Colonel, you know," I said.

"When I heard about the explosion on the boat, that reminded me of it," he said. "You know how it is when something slips your mind. Something else happens and reminds you of it."

"Sure," I said. "Something else like two innocent old people getting killed. That's some reminder, Bruno."

"I can't help it," he said. "That's what happened."

And, like a broken record, he stuck right there. Twenty minutes later, I gave up and asked, "What was the lot number on those satchel charges?"

He threw up his hands. "How the hell would *I* know? Am I an IBM machine?"

"Okay," I said. "Maybe you *are* clear on this one. But you're going to have to do something to prove it."

"Such as?"

"Get your fat ass over to the armory and get that lot number. Call it in to me at Lyon Tucker's house in the next hour. Do you read me?"

"This is my day off," he said.

"Make the sacrifice. Think of it this way: that little favor might keep you out of jail."

He was still surly, but as he let me out I could sense his relief.

Good. That was what I wanted him to feel.

There is an old trick in police interrogation called "Mutt and Jeff." Mutt is a mean bastard; he kicks the suspect around, threatens him, spits in his eye, does everything a tough cop is supposed to do. Jeff, on the other hand, is a mild, quiet guy. He argues with Mutt, pleads with him not to mistreat the prisoner. When Mutt leaves the room, Jeff commiserates with the suspect—warns him that Mutt is a psycho who might go too far one day and kill a prisoner. Between the two of them, the cops whip that poor suspect back and forth until finally, just to keep Mutt off his back, he spills everything to his buddy Jeff. Whereupon both cops laugh uproariously all the way to the courtroom.

Since I didn't have anyone to play Jeff to my Mutt, I used the business of the satchel-charge numbers as my Jeff, letting Wessel think he was getting off the hook by running a little errand. It would keep him from ducking for cover for a couple of hours, although I made a private bet that he'd think twice and then decide not to call me. That didn't matter. I wasn't interested in the numbers anyway.

There were no cars in the lot outside the Tucker house.

When Paul let me in, he said, "Miss Charity's up in her room making some telephone calls. She asked me to tell you."

"Thanks. I didn't see you at the funeral."

He looked nervous. "No sir. Someone had to take care of the house."

I went down the hall to the living room. Bethesda was there.

137

"Hello, Ben," she said. "You look like a man who wants a drink."

"Very perceptive of you," I said.

"I'd like a light scotch myself," she said. "Would you do the honors?"

"My pleasure."

I clinked ice into two glasses and made the drinks: a light one for her, a dark amber one for me.

"Charity's upstairs," she said as I handed her the glass.

"Paul told me." We touched glasses. "Health."

We spoke polite nothings, but the tension in the room seemed to grow. We drank and thus postponed what we both knew that was coming.

"Lyon tells me you're helping Miles Cooke officially now," she said.

"Uh-huh. I guess that means I ought to find another place to sleep."

"Why?"

"Because your husband is none too happy about my messing around with your business," I said. "And I can't say I really blame him. Nobody likes a house guest who suddenly turns out to be Dick Tracy."

"Don't be silly. Lyon has strong opinions, yes. But he is, and always has been a gentleman. You're our guest, and that is that."

This seemed to call for another drink. I made a new pair. We sipped.

"Mrs. Tucker—"

"Bethesda."

"Bethesda," I said. "When your husband told you about the sinking, you reacted strangely."

"Did I? I was very upset, you know. I remember being sick. I'm sorry. I usually have more backbone than that."

"That's not what I mean. If I remember correctly,

you told Lyon something like, 'Why weren't you aboard too?' Or words to that effect."

"Perhaps I did," she said. "Why is it so important?"

"I don't know. That's what I'm trying to find out."

"As nearly as I can remember," she said, "we received a call from Lyon the night before the explosion. He was up in Rockport that day. My parents were using *Channel Nine* and he said he was going to sail it back. She was rigged for solo operation, so he wouldn't have needed a crew. He often sailed alone. Obviously, I rarely sailed with him."

I went over and looked out the window at the midday glare, which seemed to flatten the town under its impact. "Who took the call, do you remember?" I asked.

"Leslie, I think. Ben, why are you asking these questions?"

"I don't know," I said truthfully. "Are you sure it was Leslie?"

"No, wait a minute," she said. "Now I remember. Paul actually took the call. Then he told Leslie what his father had said, and Leslie told me. Yes, that's the way it was."

"So everybody knew Lyon was sailing the schooner back." She nodded. "Would he have called anyone at the TV station and told them?"

"I don't know. You'll have to ask him that."

"You see what I'm getting at, don't you?"

"I think so. Someone was waiting in ambush for the boat. That meant they knew it was coming."

"Not only that," I said. "They also had to know Lyon was on board, if he was the target."

"I can't believe anyone in this house was involved."

Her glass was empty. When I took it, she noticed the burn marks on my jacket. "Lyon told me about your narrow escape," she said. "Fire bombs in the square.

139

Explosions in Shame Town. The sins of this town have been adding up, and I guess this is the showdown time. God help us, Mama and Papa's being killed was probably the beginning of it all. Ben, are there any answers?"

"I hope so," I said. "Otherwise this town's in for a real mess."

"Maybe it doesn't deserve to be saved."

"You don't mean that. A town is more than buildings and streets. Those can be replaced. People can't. Listen, Bethesda, I need all the help I can get, and I think you're holding something back. Remember, I'm on your side."

"I'd like to help, Ben," she said. "But if I'm holding something back, it's because it's not mine to give."

"If there's anything there, I'll get it sooner or later," I said.

"Perhaps you will," she said. "But that isn't the same as my telling you."

"For God's sake!" I said. "What the hell's going on? This isn't kiss and tell, you know. Your parents were *murdered!* Anyone could be next. You, your husband—even Charity."

"I don't think I know anything that would help you in this case, Ben," she said softly. "But I do know that if I spoke unwisely, I might destroy something that is very precious to me. I can't take the chance."

"I could make it official by calling Miles Cooke," I said. Good old Shock! Beat up the nice lady in her wheelchair.

The lady didn't scare worth a damn. "It wouldn't do any good," she said.

Changing direction, I said, "I noticed that you recognized George Groat this morning."

"Oh, yes," she said. "My, it's been over ten years.

140

He was just a skinny, gangling boy the last time I saw him. He's grown into a nice young man."

"That nice young man," I told her, "is known around here as Guru Goat. He runs Body and Soul, which, as you probably know, is a radical outfit suspected of causing a lot of trouble."

She smiled sadly. "Ben," she said, "to me he's just a nice young man who came to my parents' funeral."

SIXTEEN

Before I could answer, Charity came down carrying a brown manila envelope. She handed it to me. Opening it, I saw a dark, gloomy photograph of the Bijou stage in Shame Town. I recognized Guru Goat sitting under the single light hanging from the ceiling.

Charity's finger traced an area behind Guru, near the exit. A man was hurrying across the back of the stage. I took a closer look to be sure I wasn't wrong.

"It's Paul," I said.

Charity nodded. "No mistake."

"What's this?" said Bethesda. "What about Paul?"

"You tell me," I said. "What *about* Paul?"

"I don't know what you mean."

Charity started to say something, but I stopped her with a shake of my head. My eyes were riveted on Bethesda. I was operating on instinct now; the old, familiar twitch, the signal from my subconscious that it was on to something and wanted me to back off and let it run the show.

"Bethesda," I said, "who in this house conspired with Paul to get Body and Soul to murder your parents?"

There was no reaction for a moment; the question was too much for her mind to grasp and evaluate in a split second.

"Ben," Charity gasped, "are you saying—"

"I'm saying that Paul is just too widely distributed through this case for it to be coincidence. He's everywhere you look—in this house, in that Shame Town theater—even out in California. Why, Bethesda?"

She shook her head slowly. "Ben, I told you before

142

that there was something I couldn't talk about because it didn't belong to me. Well, now I see it's time to bring it out."

I looked quickly at Charity. "I'm staying!" she said.

Bethesda nodded. "She has a right to hear." Charity's stepmother stared down at her hand, which rested quietly on the arm of the wheelchair. "You're right about Paul having a special connection to the lives of this family. It goes back to California, back to the accident that put me in this chair. Paul saw what happened. He saw the whole thing."

Charity sighed and sat down slowly. Bethesda continued, "We'd been married just a few months, Lyon and I. Paul worked around the house then. He did practically eveything, but there was no formal title for his job. He was especially good with the horses, so we more or less considered him our stableman.

"On the day of my accident, he was cleaning out a stall when he saw Lyon go into the tack room and bring out my saddle, bridle, and blanket pad. Lyon saddled Flame, his favorite jumper, for me. Paul distinctly saw him pull the cinch tight. And it *was* tight. Lyon had one of his knees up against Flame's belly for leverage. Then he saddled his own horse and went inside to get me.

"Paul went back to work. When he looked up again, he saw someone at Flame's side, loosening the cinch strap." Her eyes closed wearily. "It was Leslie."

"Oh my God," said Charity.

"Paul didn't recognize what Leslie was doing. It was only later that he realized he'd been loosening the cinch. And by then it was too late. I fell on the first jump."

"But why did Leslie do it?" Charity asked.

"Pain," I said. "Anger. Hate because his mother had taken a new husband. Jealousy that some of her love was going to a strange girl. An outsider. You, baby."

Charity put an unsteady hand to her face. "But his own mother, Ben!"

"You're old enough to know that most people who are hurt get it from someone they know."

We sat there quietly for a minute. Then Bethesda began again.

"One day while I was recuperating, after we knew I wasn't going to walk again, I talked to Leslie about it. By then Paul had told me what he had seen, and I persuaded him to keep it secret. I didn't tell Leslie that Paul had seen him; I said *I* had. I asked him why. He called me a liar. Then when I pressed the truth on him he suddenly quieted down and began talking in a cold, calm voice that frightened me. He *had* done it. But he'd believed *Lyon* would be riding Flame. He hadn't thought it through any further than wanting to hurt his stepfather. And—" Her voice broke for a moment, then she went on. "And he blamed *me*, because I'd denied him, my own son, shut him out and forgotten him and his sister in my own happiness with my new marriage." She drew a long breath. "And what he said was true."

She looked at me for some kind of reaction. I didn't say anything; there wasn't much I *could* say.

"What could I do, Ben?" she asked. "I couldn't tell Lyon. He'd have killed Leslie. Literally. So when Lyon assumed he'd somehow failed to tighten the cinch properly, and asked my forgiveness. . . God help me, I let him think *he* was to blame."

"How does Paul get back into this?" I asked.

"I pleaded with him not to tell anyone what he'd seen. Then, not much later, when we came east, I was afraid to leave him behind. I didn't know what he might say if I wasn't around to watch him. He came with us, but he wanted more money. Twice what he'd

144

been getting before. I couldn't tell Lyon that, either. So I've been giving him the extra money myself."

There is a word for such goings on. But I didn't use it.

"That's it, Ben," said Bethesda. "I know I'm wrong, letting Lyon blame himself. But what is the alternative? It would destroy us all."

"This still doesn't explain what Paul was doing at Body and Soul headquarters."

"I think Bethesda's had enough for one day," said Charity. "We can get to that later."

"All right," I said, watching her push her stepmother's small, slumped figure out of the room.

I poured myself a slug of Lyon Tucker's scotch, sipped at it, and stood there worrying. Nothing seemed to be coming out right.

The door opened and Tucker came in. He grunted when he saw me, then poured himself a stiff bourbon. I decided to squeeze him the same approach I'd used on Bethesda. A crummy thing to do. But this was a crummy business.

"Mr. Tucker," I said, "it's starting to look as if the person who sank your boat lives in this house."

He put his drink down with a thump. "You're a fool," he said flatly.

I handed him the photograph. He stared at it.

"Paul?" he said. "Paul, with that hippie? Why?"

"My guess is that Paul's tied in with the Garret murders. And more than that, I think somebody else here is involved."

"Leslie!" he exploded. "That little bastard killed his grandparents just the way he tried to kill—"

He stopped, but we both knew what cat was out of which bag.

"How long have you known about Leslie loosening that cinch?" I asked.

"Right from the start. I've been a horseman all my life. When I tighten a cinch, it stays tight. Paul came to me and spilled the truth. I kept quiet because—well, I knew Leslie was after me. I wanted to protect Bethesda. So I took the blame." He gulped down a big slug of his bourbon. "It's Paul I don't understand. If he was playing a double game, he could have hit me for a bundle. Instead, he settled for an extra fifty dollars a week from me under the table."

I didn't see any point in telling him about Bethesda's additional contribution to the pot. But I did say, "There was no further hint of blackmail?"

"Not from Paul. The only real blackmailer I've been involved with is now very dead."

"Sam Bramin?"

Tucker nodded. "He came after me for a big chunk to keep another secret in the closet."

"How much?"

"A hundred and thirty thousand."

"Did you pay it?"

"Not right away. I needed time to raise it. I went to Rockport to sail *Channel Nine* back. I had a buyer for her. Then I received a call from here asking me to return immediately. So I drove down and the Garrets sailed the boat. You know what happened when they got here."

"Who telephoned you?"

"Leslie."

"Himself?"

Tucker frowned. "No, not actually. Paul spoke with me and said that Leslie had asked him to reach me and ask me to come right down, that he had to talk with me."

"Can you think of any reason Paul might have lied to you? Why he might have made that call on his own?"

"None," he said. "But I never did find Leslie when I got here. He didn't come home that night."

I had a hunch where he had slept, but I kept it to myself.

"What did you do about the blackmail?"

"I decided to pay it. Of course, Bramin wasn't stupid. He referred to it as an 'investment.'"

"In what?"

"Some years back, he and I speculated in real estate. When I learned he was deliberately driving down values in Shame Town and hurting a lot of people in the process, I broke off with him."

"So where does the blackmail come in?"

Lyon Tucker laughed bitterly. "He was smart. Every piece of documentary evidence of what happened out in Shame Town carried my signature, not his. Somehow Body and Soul found out, and that's why they've been so vindictive toward me. But no one else knows. My position in Pilgrim's Pride may not be much, Mr. Shock, but it means everything to me. I couldn't let Bramin destroy it."

"So you paid off. When?"

He took a deep breath. "Yesterday. In the middle of the afternoon."

That made him one of the last people to see Sam Bramin alive. "Did you get a receipt?" I asked.

"Don't be ridiculous." His hand shook as he poured another drink. "I gave him money and came home with my fingers crossed. Because even though I'd paid off, I knew I was under his thumb. For all I knew, he might leak those documents out of spite."

"Could you have managed a second payoff?"

He shook his head. "He stripped me," he said.

"Bramin must have been killed shortly after you left," I said. 'And that means that the killer probably has your money, because it wasn't on the premises."

Charity returned just in time to hear him say, "It's all a mess, isn't it?"

"What's a mess?" she asked. Before he could answer, she saw the photo on the table near him. "Why did you show him that, Ben?"

"Because, baby," I said, "every time I turn around, good old Paul pops up. He was doing something in cahoots with Body and Soul. He's the only link between your father and the rest of your family the night before the explosion. He told Lyon that Leslie wanted him to come back that night. But he told Leslie that your father was staying over and sailing *Channel Nine* down in the morning. Both seem to be lies."

"You make it sound very logical," she said. "All the facts fit the theory."

I was fed up. "Let's hear your better theory."

"All the facts aren't in." She turned to her father. "Daddy, Ben's been wrong before and maybe he's wrong this time."

"Let's find out," I said. "Mr. Tucker, will you get Paul in here?"

"I think I will," he said, and left.

"Charity," I said, "you are a clever girl and I love you dearly but please get the hell out of my hair!"

"You make me so mad!" she said. "Just because I suggested that someone might have been after the Garrets instead of Daddy—"

"Look, this is my *business*," I said. "I'm a professional at it. You're just a lucky amateur. You hit a couple of good ones, but you can't be right all the time."

"Oh!" she sputtered. "Oh . . . Oh!" Speechless, she stormed over to the door where she turned to deliver a furious parting line.

"Oh, *shoot!*" she yelled.

SEVENTEEN

When Lyon Tucker came back, he had some bad news.

"Paul's gone."

"Where is he?"

"I don't know."

"That does it," I said. "Check his room to see if he's taken his clothes." He hurried out and I phoned Miles Cooke. "Miles," I said, "everything here seems to point to Paul Frederick as our man."

"Who the hell is Paul Frederick?"

"Would you believe, the butler?"

He groaned. "Okay," he said. "I'll put out an all-points."

"Alert California. He's from there."

"Will do. And, Ben?"

"Yeah?"

"The firemen just got through sifting through the ashes out at the Bijou. They found part of a fuse mechanism. It's from a military demolition device called a satchel charge."

"Two of which turned up missing from the National Guard," I said. "Miles, why the hell don't you lock up Bruno Wessel?"

"Do you have a charge in mind?" he asked.

"Sheer ugliness," I said, and hung up. Tucker came back.

"He's cleaned everything out of his room," he said.

Just then I heard a familiar sound—the choking gasp the Fleetwood gives when its starter key is turned. I ran over to the window and saw my beloved car vanishing down the hill, Charity's blond hair blowing out the open window.

"Your daughter," I told Tucker, "has just stolen my car."

"In that case," he said, "have another drink."

I did. So did he.

"What now?" he asked.

"They'll catch up with Paul sooner or later," I said. "Meanwhile, it would be nice if we could find the link between the Bramin and Garret killings."

"How?"

"Money, maybe. You usually find it at the bottom of killings. Money and malice. Maybe a little madness. The three big M's they taught us about in the Police Academy." I looked at him hopefully. "Tell me it wasn't cash you gave him. Tell me it was a check."

"Cash."

Hope never dies. "But you made a list of the numbers?"

"There wasn't time. I had to get it from four different banks."

"Forgive me for saying it," I said, "but for a smart man, you can sometimes be very stupid."

"I know," he said, shaking his head. I stood up. "Where are you going?"

"I've sweated through this shirt," I said. "I'll put on a fresh one and you can run me downtown. I'll borrow a car from Cooke."

I left him sitting there, looking as if someone had knocked the wind out of him.

While I was changing my shirt, the doorbell rang. Then I heard voices arguing. I went to the head of the stairs. Tucker was saying, "I don't give a damn, I'm not going anywhere with you."

Are you ready to hear what a guy who has just finished calling someone *else* stupid does next?

I went down to see what was happening without taking my .38. Very bright.

Tucker and Henry Koos were standing in the hallway. Koos had his own service revolver out, trained on Tucker. I started to sneak back up the stairway, but he saw me.

"Come on down, city boy," he called, waving his hardware in my direction. It was very convincing. I came on down.

"What's going on?" I asked.

"I'm taking your friend in," he said.

"On what charge?"

"Murder will do."

"This is a local matter," I said. "If you've got evidence, turn it over to Cooke. He'll handle things."

"Oh, I've got evidence," he said. "This *gentleman's* prints were all over that pier."

"That's enough evidence to bring him in for questioning," I said. "Not enough to pull an arrest."

"How about a little item in the trunk of his car?" Koos waved the gun. "Come on out and take a peek."

The trunk of the white Continental was open. Nestled down inside it, wrapped in a plastic bag, was a satchel charge.

Tucker's face went white. "Ben," he said, "I honest to God never saw that thing before. I haven't opened this trunk in weeks."

"Sure," said Koos. "That bomb just grew there." His own car was parked beside the Continental, engine running. "Get in," he told Tucker.

"Hold on," I said. "I'll call Chief Cooke."

"Cooke's the one who told me to make the pinch," Koos said. "So keep your nose out of this, Shock."

I looked at Lyon Tucker. His arms hung limp, all resistance gone.

"Lyon," I asked him, "don't you have any explanation for this?"

"I never saw that thing before," he repeated.

"Okay, Koos," I said. "Take him down to the station. Tell Cooke I'll be along in a couple of minutes."

"Tell him yourself," he said. Tucker got into the car with him. The patrol car scratched gravel and headed down the hill.

I went inside and dialed Cooke's office. He wasn't in. I got the desk sergeant.

"This is Ben Shock," I said. "How long ago did Cooke okay a pickup on Lyon Tucker?"

"It didn't come through my desk," he said. "First I heard of it. He'll be back in an hour or so—"

That was as far as he got. I hung up and ran for Tucker's car. I left the satchel charge in the trunk, slammed the lid, ripped out the keys, and piled into the front seat.

And *then* I remembered my .38. Back into the house, up the stairs, into the bedroom. I jammed the pistol into my hip pocket, and scooted down the stairs again. By the time I had fired up the Continental, Koos was already out of sight. At the bottom of the hill, the road branched three ways. The middle road went into Pilgrim's Pride. The left branch went up the coast toward Rockport, the right one toward Gloucester. I didn't have to worry about the middle one, because if Koos really was taking Tucker to the station, there was nothing to be alarmed about.

Then Charity appeared in the Fleetwood at the intersection, coming from the Gloucester direction. I leaned out the window and yelled, "Did you see a state police car going that way?"

"No," she said, surprised. "But—"

I didn't take time to figure out what the "but" would have been. I turned left and floored it. By the time I hit the next curve I was doing sixty-five. In the rear-view mirror, I saw the Fleetwood take off after me.

When I reached the outskirts of town I really let her out. Far ahead, I saw the police car. As I closed in on it, I saw that it was parked on the shoulder near a clump of trees. I swooped in behind it and shut off the engine.

The police car was empty. That left the trees.

Koos was too busy to see me coming.

He had Tucker backed up against a big oak, and was jabbing the pistol into his stomach. He was asking Tucker something. Every time Tucker shook his head, Koos jammed the pistol deeper into the older man's stomach. When Tucker doubled over, the state cop gave him a savage backhand blow across the face.

I slipped out my own pistol, and moved a little closer. When Koos let Tucker have it again, I yelled, "Hold it right there, Koos. Freeze!"

His arm had been swinging for another blow and he converted its energy into a sideway dive that took him halfway behind a charred stump. His pistol started coming up in my direction and I shouted, "Don't!"

He did. I don't know where his bullet went, but when I aimed at his shoulder my pistol threw high and to the side and the slug took off the top of his head.

Tucker staggered over toward me, blood running down his face.

"Watch out—" he gasped. "He'll kill—"

Sickened, I said, "He won't kill anybody."

There came a screeching of brakes and I looked up to see Charity running toward us.

"Daddy!" she cried. "What's wrong?"

"He was trying to make me tell where the money

153

is," Tucker said to me, choking. "He said if I told him he'd leave me alone."

Then the entire police force of Pilgrim's Pride arrived, Miles Cooke in the lead. He looked at the crumpled body and went white.

"The desk sergeant radioed me something funny was going on," he said. "Jesus! What happened?"

"My goddamned gun threw high."

"Did you *have* to kill him?"

"No, damn it!" I yelled. "I could have been a nice guy and let him kill *me!* Listen, Miles, this character kidnapped Tucker. He had him up against that tree, beating the living crap out of him. I arrived and he started shooting. I shot back. I was lucky. He wasn't. What the hell do you want from me?"

"It's the truth," said Tucker. "Koos said he was arresting me. But instead of taking me to the station, he brought me out here and started beating up on me."

"Did you authorize a pickup on Tucker?" I asked.

"Of course not," said Cooke.

"Well, Koos told me he had one."

"This case gets messier every minute," said Cooke. "That seventy-five-millimeter we were sitting on?"

"Yeah?" But I knew what was coming.

"It's gone," Cooke said. "We pulled up the rope and found an empty loop. Somebody swam out underwater and swiped our evidence."

"This looks like a day for folks to play fast and loose with the heavy artillery," I said. "Take a look at what's in the trunk of Tucker's car."

Cooke's men lifted the satchel charge out gingerly, trying not to disturb any fingerprints.

"Lyon," said Cooke, "I'll need a statement." Then, looking at Tucker's battered face, "There's no rush. Any time today."

"I'll get cleaned up and see you later," Tucker promised. He got behind the wheel of the Continental. I started to get in beside him, but he protested, "No, no. I can drive."

I got into the Fleetwood, Charity beside me.

"You drive," she said. "I've got things to tell you."

"Amateur luck again?" I muttered, starting the engine.

"As opposed to your professional skill," she said. "Ben, thank God for that professional skill. If you hadn't been here—"

"Chalk it up to my instant dislike of Koos," I said. "If I hadn't hated him so much I might have shrugged and let him take your father in without thinking twice. Seeing that satchel charge in the trunk was pretty impressive evidence." I turned the car back toward town. "Now, suppose you tell me where you've been."

"Talking with Guru," she said. "I wasn't satisfied with your sinister motives for Paul."

"So the little lamb walks into the lion's den. Great."

"Oh, Ben! Guru—George—may be militant, but he's an old friend. And there's nothing sinister at all. Paul's his *uncle*. He's been trying to talk George into stopping the hippie bit. That's his only connection with Body and Soul."

Good old Paul. The traditional red herring to draw the brilliant detective off the scent. Agatha Christie would have given me an "F."

"As for Guru," Charity went on, "he swears he had nothing to do with sinking Daddy's boat. And while he said he wishes he'd thought of trying to frame Sam Bramin and the Defenders, it never occurred to him until I mentioned it."

I groaned. "And you believed him, just like that?"

"Just like that," she said. "Now don't get mad

because I spilled your ideas to him. Ben, we just couldn't leave it up in the air. I had to know about Paul."

I sighed. "I hope you're right, baby."

"Guru said Paul called him this morning and said he was going home. He just got fed up with everything and wanted out."

"You make a good sale, honey," I said. "I'll phone Miles and call off the hounds on Paul. So now we're back where we started, with three murders and no likely suspects."

"I know. But that's better than arresting the wrong man, isn't it?"

"Yes," I said. "That's true."

The turn for the road leading back up to the Tucker house came before I expected it. I was rolling fast, so I had to brake hard. There was a crash from the trunk. I edged the car off the road and stopped.

"What was that?" Charity asked. "It sounded like the transmission fell out."

"It might have been the SCUBA tank," I said. "But I had it lashed down."

When the trunk lid went up I saw the air tank tumbled over in one corner. It—and all my other diving gear—was wet. I tasted the water. Salty.

Just like the harbor that Cooke said the 75 had disappeared from.

EIGHTEEN

That night, as Charity and I tied into a pair of gargantuan Rockport lobsters, I said, "The question is, who's got your Daddy's hundred and thirty thou? Find him and you find the one who compressed Sam Bramin."

This evening was far from a celebration. After we had all made our statements that afternoon, Miles Cooke had taken me aside and said, "Ben, I'm going to have to relieve you of your deputy spot. State is willing to accept the possibility that Koos was a bad apple. But they won't sit still for your carrying a badge until the investigation's over. I'm sorry. You've been a real help. But it would have to be the same even if you were one of my permanent men."

I understood. I didn't feel any too happy about what had happened anyway. I was starting to wonder if maybe Captain Murphy was right. Maybe I ought to think more and shoot less. Although I didn't know what good thinking would have done me if I had tried it while Koos was blasting lead at me.

"Poor Ben," Charity said, touching my hand on the candlelit table. "You relax after one mess and find yourself up to your neck in another one."

"A policeman's lot is not a happy one," I said.

"Sometimes you start wondering," she said, "what does it matter? Who *cares* who's guilty? Finding the villain won't bring back the dead."

"True enough," I said. "But it might keep him from making any more people dead. Look, baby, I know I get mad sometimes—and personally involved—and I

157

shouldn't. I'm not in the punishment racket, even though that's what it looks like sometimes. What I'm really trying to do is keep nasty things from happening to nice people, and part of the way to do that is to take the thugs and the hoods off the streets. Locking them up isn't a cure, but it's all we've got. Too bad we can't borrow the magic operation a pulp magazine hero named Doc Savage had. He'd cut some deep brain nerve and from then on his nasties became Mr. Nice Guys." I sipped at my martini and sighed. "Meanwhile, honey, it is ten of eleven and I am fresh out of clues, besides which Cooke made me turn in my badge. What do you say we go home and sit upon the widow's walk and rub noses?"

But it was occupied. Leslie was there, staring down the hill at the floodlights shining on Tucker Field a couple of hundred yards below the house.

"Sorry," I said, turning to go back inside.

"Oh, shove it!" he said, brushing past us.

When he was out of earshot, I said, "Forgive me, my love, but your brother is not the most likable person."

"Shhh," she said.

For a while we played Eskimo, rubbing noses, then tummies. Her breathing got heavier.

I drew back, kissed her gently, and said, "Before Shock gets too shook, we'd better go beddy-bye. Separately." And I gave her a brotherly kiss.

She gave me a definitely nonsisterly kiss in return. "You must be frigid," she whispered. Then, before I could answer, she gave me a sweet, gentle kiss, that told me she knew I had stopped just before she began to tense up. "Darling Ben," she said. "Goodnight."

She went downstairs and I had a cigarette while I pulled myself together. Then I went to my empty room, stripped, and went to bed. But there were too many thoughts flitting around in my skull for sleep to come easily, so I just lay there, slowly getting drowsy. My mental night watchman must have dozed off, though, because the first signal I got that someone had joined me in bed was a finger moving along the inside of my thigh.

A familiar scent told me that my bedmate was none other than Scarlett O'Hara Tucker.

"Shhh," she said. "Don't yell."

The warning wasn't necessary. The last thing I wanted then was an interested witness. Particularly Charity.

"What are you doing here?" I whispered. Come to think of it, it *was* a stupid question.

"I came to apologize," she said, her finger tracing a path along my chest. Gone were both the phony Mason-Dixon accent and the growl she'd used to call me "Bastard!" Now she was gentle, feminine, and touchingly sweet. "Mother told me everything you've been doing—you and Charity. How you stopped that man from killing Lyon. How you had to shoot to save your own life. That must have been awful for you."

"It's a living," I said.

"Then she told me the truth about that riding accident. She told me about Leslie, too."

Scarlett seemed to have a lot to get off her chest, so I kept quiet. Especially since her chest was snuggled so cozily up against mine.

"I've been such a smug little bitch," she said. "I thought Lyon was a monster—that he'd crippled my mother. So I conspired with Leslie to make life miserable for him. But I'll make it up to Daddy. I've got a lot of making up to do. A lot," she breathed in my ear.

When my voice came it sounded more like Donald

Duck than Ben Shock. "Scarlett, I want you out of this bed right now!"

"Do you?"

I knew if she wasn't gone in ten seconds, my willpower would be. So what's wrong with that? asked the little lecher in my head. "Please, Scarlett," I said. "Be a good kid."

She sighed. "All right, Ben. If you insist."

She stood, making a delightful silhouette against the dim light of the window. "Do you know those things I said about being better than Charity? I lied. How could I know I was better when I haven't even tried?"

While I was digesting that, she leaned forward in the darkness and kissed my neck, breathing one word—"Yet!" And then was gone.

My dreams, when I finally went to sleep, were very, very interesting.

NINETEEN

Next morning, I discovered where all the Body and Soul had been hiding.

The bleachers around Tucker Field were filled with tourists and townspeople, while the high school band tootled through a series of Sousa marches.

I had about as much interest in viewing a reenactment of Pilgrim's Pride's gallant defense against the redskins as I did in swimming in that rotten cold harbor again. But Charity wanted to see it, so there we were. When things were almost ready to start, she began wondering where her father was. I offered to drive her up the hill, but she said the car was jammed in and it would be quicker to walk. I stayed in the bleachers to hold our seats and she took off.

It was far more interesting watching her magnificent behind switching up the slope than looking at the mock soldiers forming ragged ranks on the field, so I devoted myself to that pleasantry until she was out of sight.

The loudspeaker droned out the glorious history of Pilgrim's Pride. The phony Colonial soldiers began to dress up their ranks. I recognized Bull Martin out in front, attired as the legendary Captain John Cross. Directly behind him was Bruno Wessel, cutting a hilarious figure in red coat and silk pantaloons. He looked like a circus bear, complete with everything except the little umbrella.

Many of the faces in the ranks had a staunch, American Defender look about them.

The band blew a couple of flourishes, and the unseen announcer told us how one autumn day the peaceful village had come under attack by hostile Indians.

Ten moth-eaten teen-agers portraying hostile Indians straggled out of the woods.

"The savage onslaught was met bravely by the village's defenders," said the loudspeaker. I looked up the hill, wondering where the hell Charity was. Then I heard a gasp from the crowd and turned my eyes back to the field.

The teen-aged savages were fleeing for their lives. The brave defenders began huddling together for warmth.

Out of the woods came at least thirty hippies, all wearing war paint and headdresses around their long hair. I remembered Guru warning Wessel that on the Fourth of July the Indians might turn out to be the good guys. It looked like he was making good on his threat. The "Indians" marched up to the quavering ranks of Colonial troops.

The announcer decided the show must go on. "Negotiations failed," he said. "And so the Indian nation struck."

The crowd was anything but convinced that this was a peaceable reenactment. Those nearest the edges of the bleachers began to slip away toward their cars.

Doggedly, the announcer followed his script: "Then Black Pony attacked Captain John Cross."

Except Black Pony, whom I recognized as Guru Goat, wasn't interested in Captain Cross. Guru passed Bull Martin and stood in front of Bruno Wessel, who raised his phony musket like a club. Guru lifted his tomahawk.

The long-awaited confrontation between Body and Soul and the American Defenders was playing to a packed house.

The high school band frantically launched into "Columbia, Gem of the Ocean."

I began gandy-dancing down the shaky rows of bleachers.

There came a familiar *whooshing* sound and a pillar of earth and smoke burst from the turf of the playing field. Somebody was shooting off a goddamned recoilless rifle again!

People screamed.

Other people fell down, bleeding.

The brave defenders broke and ran. All except Guru and Bruno Wessel, who were locked in desperate combat.

Another *whoosh*. A second round. This explosion picked up the two combatants and threw them into a heap ten feet away.

One of the bodies stirred and began crawling away, dragging bleeding legs over the grass. It was Guru.

The other figure would never move again. Bruno's meaty body had absorbed most of the blast. He was cut nearly in two.

People pointed. My eyes followed their fingers.

High on top of the Tucker house, planted firmly on the widow's walk, someone raised a stovepipe-like device. It belched flame and the crowd screamed as another shell burned its way toward us. This one overshot and tore up ten yards of parking lot.

Where the hell was Miles Cooke? Like they say, there's never a cop when you need one.

A police sergeant shouted orders. His men formed up, aiming their pistols at the distant figure. They would have been more successful throwing rocks. Suddenly it all fell into place for me. I'd had the information and misread it. I knew who it was up there on the widow's walk.

I had to get to the house. I looked around again for Cooke. He still wasn't anywhere in sight.

The quickest route was right up the exposed road. I hoped the marksman wouldn't be able to hit a running figure with the clumsy 75.

He couldn't, but he tried. One round burst a few feet behind me. The hot blast picked me up and tumbled me head over heels on the blazing asphalt, and my last good suit went to that Great Robert Hall's in the Sky.

The marksman gave up trying to kill me with the recoilless and switched to an automatic rifle. Now I had to run for my life. Slugs pockmarked the asphalt on both sides of me. Rocks and gravel peppered me, and twice I was sure I had been hit. I had a strong urge to throw myself down and try to dig a hole, but that would have been sure suicide.

I finally got close enough to the house so he couldn't depress the gun enough to hit me. So he raised it and concentrated on the cops who were following me up the hill. A frantic scream told me he'd had better luck with his new targets.

The front door was locked. I tried to kick it down and almost broke my foot. So I poked my pistol through the window glass, raked out one pane, and unlocked the catch. I shoved the window up and climbed in, crunching broken glass under my shoe.

This part of the house was dark and gloomy. I kept my .38 at the ready and vaulted up the stairs. On the second floor, as I crept down the hall, I heard muffled pounding inside one of the bedrooms. There was a key on the hall carpet. I tried it and the door opened.

Inside, Bethesda was slumped in her wheelchair, dazed. Scarlett huddled on the bed. And Charity, who had been pounding on the door, let go with a roundhouse swing that would have taken off an ear, had it connected. I ducked and she smashed her knuckles against the wall.

"Hold on!" I yelled. "It's me! Where's your father?"

She didn't seem to hear me. "Oh, Ben!" she cried. "He's gone insane."

Privately, I figured he had been insane for quite a while. But he was still up there firing away and as long as he had that automatic rifle he didn't have any sympathy coming from me.

I headed for the stairs. Charity ran the other way, toward the living room.

The door to the steps leading to the widow's walk was open. Carefully, I peered around it.

A barrage of automatic rifle slugs chewed up the wall. I ducked and pegged two shots up the stairwell. He answered with another burst. I ducked again and let two more rounds go blindly. Now I had only two bullets left. I would have to save them for a target I could see.

Outside, a fusillade of shots sounded. I heard him firing back and chanced rushing the stairs while he was busy with the police below.

I got halfway up the stairs when the ugly muzzle of the automatic rifle poked back down in my direction. I dropped and squeezed off one of my remaining shots. It missed. The rifle slugs began chewing up the wall above my head. I tried the second shot. I knew I'd connected, because the automatic rifle stopped firing for a moment. But now I was dry. I fumbled out the Philippine fighting knife and began scuttling up the stairs.

The ugly muzzle reappeared and sweat broke out all over my body. He stood at the head of the stairs, swaying slightly. Blood dripped down the front of his shirt. He was out on his feet. If I could wait two minutes, he would be dead.

But in two minutes, *I* might be. He was gone, but he wanted to take me with him.

The rifle trembled, pointed at my stomach.

I threw the knife. It missed and stuck, quivering, in the door jamb.

The rifle barrel steadied, aiming right at my belt buckle. I gathered my strength for a last, desperate dive.

Behind me, Charity's voice screamed, "Ben! *Get down!*"

I plastered myself against the steps. Something went *Boom!* and Leslie O'Hara Tucker was hurled back, through the door and over the railing of the widow's walk.

When I slid down the stairs, Charity stood there, the ornate shotgun I'd seen in the living room dangling loosely from her hand. Gently, I took it away from her.

"God help me, Ben," she said. "He's *insane*. I had to do it."

Sobbing, she pressed against me. I stroked her hair.

A distant thumping finally penetrated my consciousness, and I went across the hall and released Lyon Tucker from the closet in which he'd been locked.

TWENTY

Every society has its own version of the dark destroyer. In Africa, it is Fisi—the hyena. To those who snicker at Fisi inside the cages of zoos, it would be a revelation to learn that in certain parts of the world the hyena is feared more than the most ferocious lion. Fisi means death. Fisi is a grotesque creature the Creator gave a laughing snout and permanently crippled hindquarters. Though he has jaws that can crush a coconut, the hyena is still unable to run down the slowest of game. So Fisi lives on the aged and infirm; he destroys the weak and the lame. He is a devout coward; even a determined woodchuck can drive him away. But let a lion be weak with some illness and Fisi will kill him.

The New York Police Department has its Fisis too. Hyenas who wait until you are down, until you are blind or crippled.

They had been waiting for me. Now it was time for them to make their move.

The State of Massachusetts pressed no charges against me for the death of Koos. That didn't matter to the Fisi. "Gun-happy" and "kill-crazy" were two of the politest labels they pinned on me.

Captain Murphy wanted to stand behind me. It wouldn't have worked. I resigned before anyone but me got hurt.

But the Fisi can raise doubts in your own mind.

Was I too fast with the gun? In every case, I had seen no other alternative. And I had not aimed to kill.

But when I fired, my bullet always seemed to find the vital spot instead of wounding.

I was sick and tired, and knew if I stayed in the city any longer I'd wind up back at the station for beating some surly cab driver's brains out.

When I am fed up with the world, when life seems more trouble than it's worth, I escape to a little place in upstate New York named Lake Chenango, and I sit in a rowboat there and fish for bass that never take my lure, and drink a lot of beer and get sunburned.

Now, two weeks after the disastrous Fourth of July holiday, I sat in my rowboat sipping a Utica Club beer and letting the sun toast my peeling nose.

I heard the rumble of an engine. When I looked up I saw a large cruiser rounding the headland of my private inlet. It made me mad. I know that I don't own the whole lake, that there is a big chunk out there that services millions of tourists and boats and even water skiers, but my inlet had always been out of their path. Now civilization was moving in on me. I could see I was going to have to find another lake.

The boat headed straight for me. Great. Some punk wanted to see if he could swamp me with his bow wave. I hauled in my line and made ready to heave a full can of beer at the bastard.

But he cut his engine and coasted up alongside with scarcely a ripple.

"Come aboard," said Miles Cooke.

I stared at him. Then Charity came out of the wheelhouse and gave me a big grin.

"I bet," she said, "that our beer is colder than your beer."

I climbed aboard. "This goddamned lake was supposed to be a secret. Somebody named Murphy has a big mouth."

Charity handed me a can of Schaefer. It *was* colder than mine.

"You're a hard man to find," said Cooke.

"I meant to be," I said. Charity looked away.

"I hear you quit the Department," Cooke said. "I can use a good man. How about it?"

"Really?" I said. "Is Pilgrim's Pride in the market for a trigger-happy, kill-crazy washout?"

"Benjamin Lincoln Shock!" said Charity. "Stop feeling sorry for yourself."

"I'm not feeling sorry for myself. Just mad at a lot of other people." I took a swig of the beer. And mad at myself. I pulled some beauties. If I'd been smarter, a couple of men might still be alive."

"My, my, my," said Miles Cooke. "You *are* an empty-head. You merely tracked down the connection between Leslie and Bruno Wessel. You only tied Guru Goat in with George Groat. . . ."

"Give credit where it's due," I said. "Charity came up with that one. Her and her little camera." I toasted my beer can at her. "A real natural," I said. "Walking proof that a lucky, talented amateur can beat an unlucky, dumb pro any day of the week."

"You know we found Lyon's money hidden inside the door panel of Leslie's car," said Cooke. "Any theories on that? Do you suppose he killed Bramin just for money?"

I shook my head. "No, the money was incidental," I said, looking at Charity.

"It's all right, Ben," she said. "Go on."

"You can't blame yourself," I told her. "He was dead on his feet. He just hadn't fallen down."

"I shot him," she said calmly, "and I'd do it again. The least you could be is grateful. He was getting ready to turn you into Swiss Cheese."

The tone of her voice cheered me. I knew she must

169

still be deeply disturbed, but being able to joke about it seemed healthy.

"Come on, Ben," said Cooke. "Loosen up. My curiosity's killing me. You left town so fast, I never did get the whole story."

"It was the same old series of lousy breaks," I said. "Sam Bramin came to town and brought Bruno Wessel. That was bad news for Leslie, who was already pretty mixed up anyway. He met Bruno. They became friends."

"Don't soft-soap the troops, Ben," said Charity. "I know all about Leslie. I just didn't like to talk about it. He and Bruno became lovers."

"Okay," I said. "Right from the start, Bramin was feathering his nest so he'd have a soft place to fall. He was looking ahead to when he'd be ready to cut out."

"Taking Bruno Wessel with him," Charity said dryly. "So poor Leslie had to do something or his boyfriend would have been off for parts unknown."

"Right," I said. "Leslie couldn't join the Defenders —they wouldn't have him. And I guess he didn't want to be a camp follower. But then he got an idea. He remembered his boyhood buddy, George Groat back in California, who was now making a name for himself in hippie activities as Guru Goat. Leslie gave him a sad story about how Pilgrim's Pride needed his leadership more than California. So Guru came east and set up Body and Soul."

Cooke popped me another beer. "I know that part of the story," he said. "There was the riot, and from then on the people in town felt caught between Sam Bramin's devil and Guru's deep blue sea. Property values kept going down in Shame Town, and Sam Bramin kept buying. I ran a check last week. That bastard owned half of the area."

"And he was getting ready to grab off the other half," I said. "But he needed cash. He had a dirty hold on Lyon, with forged documents that Lyon would have one hell of a time disproving." I frowned. "That's one thing Lyon held back from me; the other half of the blackmail scheme. Bramin also threatened to reveal that it was Leslie who had brought Body and Soul to town."

"But why blow up *Channel Nine?*" Charity asked. "That could have been turned into more money."

"Bramin thought your father was stalling, so he put pressure on Leslie too. He threatened to send Wessel away if Lyon didn't kick in." I chose my words carefully. "Leslie must have been stumbling along the crumbling edge of the mental cliff for years. And this threat from Bramin gave him a hard shove. Leslie couldn't lose Wessel. And he knew he stood to inherit the Tucker Enterprises stock from his grandparents. So when Lyon went up to Rockport to pick up the Garrets, Leslie went into action. He knew Body and Soul had a seventy-five, and he put the heist on it. Then he suckered Paul into making a phone call, calling Tucker back from Rockport. And he told the family he'd received a second call from Tucker, saying he'd be sailing the boat back the next morning.

"Leslie sneaked out on Bramin's dock and sank *Channel Nine*, then stashed the seventy-five off the pier. By this time, he owed no loyalty to George Groat at all. He knew that when the weapon was found, the serial numbers would trace it right to Body and Soul." I shook my head. "Except a dumb New York cop forgot to copy down the numbers until it was too late."

Charity shuddered. "It's horrible," she said.

"Worse than that, it was pointless. I would guess that when Leslie told Bramin that he'd get pocket money and little else from his inheritance, Bramin gave the kid his walking papers. But Leslie must have around, seen his stepfather pay the blackmail money, and then Leslie put a gun on Bramin to force him into his own baling machine."

"Revenge?" said Cooke.

"Revenge and profit," I said. "Leslie thought that with Bramin out of the way, he'd be able to buy Wessel lock, stock, and barrel. He was probably right, too."

"And the explosion at the Bijou Theater?" Charity asked.

That was part of Bramin's dirty works, which is what threw me off track. It had nothing at all to do with the Garret murders. Wessel was under orders from Bramin to keep the heat on in Shame Town, and there's nothing like a good big explosion to drive property values down."

I saw a flash as a bass took an insect off the lake's surface. Smart bastard, I thought; he doesn't show up until I'm too busy yakking to put a hook into him.

"Anyway," I went on, "my visit to Wessel scared the hell out of him, and he told Leslie to take his little Triumph and vanish. Bruno feared exposure more than he liked money. By now, Leslie was way over the edge anyway, so he decided to clean house. The Defenders had cheated him of his boyfriend, and like the typical jealous lover, he decided on revenge. He knew the seventy-five was still stashed off the end of the pier. He also knew we had a guard on it. That came from living in the same house with a loud-mouthed cop who bragged a lot." Charity smiled, and I went on. "So he borrowed my SCUBA gear, swam out and got the seventy-five, dried it off, and stashed it upstairs.

"Meanwhile, Wessel had leaked the story of the

blackmail payoff to Koos, who figured Tucker still had the money. So Koos planted the extra satchel charge to give him an excuse to rough Lyon up." I shook my finger at Miles Cooke. "You've got some bad boys in your town."

"Koos was a Boston boy," he said.

"Well, he was an unlucky one," I said, pouring my warm beer over the side. *That* would fix those smart-ass bass. "Okay, we're up to the Fourth of July. Leslie locked up everybody in the house at gunpoint with an automatic rifle he'd lifted from his boyfriend's private stash. He had his faithless lover to aim at, a not inconsiderable target, and he connected. Then his own luck ran out for good." I studied the empty beer can. "Like mine."

Charity fumbled in her purse. "Luck changes all the time," she said, handing me a small pasteboard card.

I read it: "Shock and Tucker, Investigations."

"What the hell is this?" I asked.

"It's actually the Chief's idea," she said.

Cooke explained: "Sometimes in the law business a town's own law can tangle it up. But you came swinging in, a lot of spit hit the fan, and eventually the mess got cleaned up. I think it's a service quite a few towns would like to have on tap." He waved a hand. "Oh," he hurried to add, "not that any of them would ever admit to it in public. But privately, I can assure you that I know at least a dozen places whose solid citizens would like very much to talk with the likes of Shock and Tucker."

"I'm through with the cop business," I said.

"What else do you know how to do?"

I shrugged.

Charity said, "What else do you know that you and I could do together?"

173

"You are a lucky, talented amateur," I said.

"I had a phone call from a friend of mine in Kentucky," she said. "Do you know anything about race horses?"

"Not a damned thing."

"You could learn."

"Honey," I said, "I'm exhausted. I wouldn't be any good to anybody."

"In that case, what do you have to lose?"

I sighed.

"Nothing," I said.

are you missing out on some great Pyramid books?

You can have any title in print at Pyramid delivered right to your door! To receive your Pyramid Paperback Catalog, fill in the label below (use a ball point pen please) and mail to Pyramid . . .

PYRAMID PUBLICATIONS
Mail Order Department
9 Garden Street
Moonachie, New Jersey 07074

NAME_____

ADDRESS_____

CITY_____ STATE_____

P-5 _____ ZIP_____